Glitter &
Sparkle

Shari L. Tapscott

Glitter & Sparkle
Glitter & Sparkle Series, Book 1

Copyright © 2016 by Shari L. Tapscott
All rights reserved.

ISBN-13: 978-1540773722
ISBN-10: 1540773728

Editing by Donna Rich & Z.A. Sunday
Cover Design by Shari L. Tapscott

Contemporary Fiction

Just the Essentials
Glitter & Sparkle
Shine & Shimmer

The Eldentimber Series

Pippa of Lauramore
Grace of Vernow: An Eldentimber Novelette
Anwen of Primewood
Seirsha of Errinton
Rosie of Triblue: An Eldentimber Novella
Audette of Brookraven

Fairy Tale Kingdoms

Puss without Boots: A Puss in Boots Retelling
Chains of Gold: A Fairy Tale Kingdoms Novelette

For Chelsea

Forward Chelsea Army! Sparkle! Sparkle!

Chapter One
November 1st

Glitter is the most fabulous thing ever created. With a little spray-on adhesive, you can literally stick it to anything. That's why I've covered my lamp, bookshelf, wall art, and virtually everything on my desk in the stuff.

These aren't kindergarten craft projects, either. If anyone can wield a glue gun and a paintbrush with a bit of finesse, it's me. Just ask anyone who follows my blog. (And not to brag, but there are a lot of people you could ask, if you know what I mean.)

"Lauren, it's time for dinner," Mom yells up the stairs.

I'm staring at a new owl figurine I bought at the mall yesterday, trying to decide what I'm going to do with it. It's white, completely boring, but it has so much potential, I just had to pick it up. Idly, I run a

1

comb through my hair as I think over my options.

"Now, Lauren!"

Sighing, I step back from my desk. Parents, or maybe just my parents, don't understand how the artistic muse works. I can't just stop for dinner. I need to create.

I roll my eyes as soon as the thought crosses my mind because it's a tiny bit dramatic, even for me.

After quickly pulling my mess of honey-colored curls in a quick ponytail, I snatch the owl and trot down the stairs and into the kitchen.

"I think it needs to be hot pink," I announce to no one in particular as I plop into my regular seat and set the owl beside my plate. "But I've used it so much lately, it's feeling overdo—"

I gurgle to an abrupt stop. Sitting directly across from me, in my repulsive older brother's regular seat, is the hottest guy I've seen in my life.

And I have no idea who he is.

"Hey." His mouth twists into a sideways smile, and he looks as if he's trying not to laugh at me.

"Who are you?" I blurt out.

Stupid, stupid, Lauren. When a hot guy says "hey," you say "hey" back.

"You remember Harrison." Mom comes up behind him and places her hand affectionately on his shoulder.

No way.

This gorgeous, slightly rumple-haired, lean-muscled Greek gladiator is Brandon's moron friend who used to make rude noises with his armpit?

Impossible.

Harrison's eyes light with amusement. "You have paint on your cheek."

As I swipe at my face with a napkin, I inwardly groan and curse. (Not really bad words, mind you. I'm a lady.)

"Just like old times," he adds, obviously enjoying my discomfort.

What Harrison—and it must be Harrison after all—is referring to, is the day he and Brandon attacked me with Rustic Red paint a summer long, long ago when my parents made us update the shed.

I was ten, so the boys were thirteen. Harrison moved to Connecticut the year after that, and I have never been so happy to see someone leave the neighborhood. Mom, who's been friends with his mother her whole life, wasn't so happy.

"What are you doing here?" I ask rather rudely.

I don't care if he's now the hottest thing to ever grace our kitchen table—he's Harrison. And I don't like him.

Mom shoots me a look. "Harrison's transferring to the university, and I told Vanna he could live with us for a couple months until he finds a place."

How is this something my parents forgot to tell me? How do you not toss that into a conversation at some point? *Lauren, we're so proud of you for landing the lead in the play, and, by the way, Brandon's obnoxious friend is going to be living with us for a few months.*

"He'll be staying in the guest house," Mom continues.

"The guest house?" I ask, incredulous.

It's my craft studio, the place I film the videos for my blog. All of my art stuff is out there.

It's my space.

Instead of answering, Mom shoots me another look and sets a pan of lasagna on the table. Her fabulous garlic bread sits next to it, all buttered and browned to perfection. Sadly, I've lost my appetite.

Dad strides into the room and plucks a piece of bread from the plate. As Mom scolds him, I scowl at my owl, refusing to look at the newly gorgeous interloper across from me.

"Deb texted and said you got in early," Dad says to Harrison as he takes a seat. "How was the weather?"

"It was just fine, sir," Harrison says. "Thank you for letting me stay here for a bit."

Suck up.

"Not a problem," Dad says. "We're happy to have you again. You practically used to live here."

Ugh. I just...I can't do this. I start to stand, already forming excuses. I'll fake a migraine or girl problems or...pneumonia or something.

As I'm rising, Mom says, "Lauren. *Sit.*"

Like a well-trained dog, I plop back in my seat and glare at her. For a brief moment, she shoots me an understanding look. Mom knows I never liked Harrison. He wasn't like some of Brandon's other friends who were actually nice to me. He was awful.

With no escape from the table, I let my mind wander. Why couldn't it have been Austin staying with us? He was Brandon's best friend in high school, and not only was he incredibly cute, but he also had manners. Oooh...or Jamie. I'll never forget the summer he and Brandon hung out at the basketball court...

"We moved your stuff to the garage," Dad says, and when there's a hush at the table, it becomes obvious he's talking to me.

Horrified, I look up at him. "The *garage?*"

"You didn't think I would share, huh?" he says, missing my meaning entirely. "I moved things around and made room for you. You're welcome, Princess."

Harrison watches the exchange, and amusement shines in his ocean blue eyes.

Ocean blue eyes? Where did that come from? Like I care what color his eyes are.

I look at my plate and cut a large, flat noodle with

my fork. Normally, I would stuff the whole thing in my mouth, but it's weird having Harrison here, sitting across from me, studying me for weaknesses he can prey upon later.

"So, Lauren, you're a senior this year?" Harrison asks.

Of course, I've just taken a bite. Silence descends over the table while I chew. Why does food become dryer when everyone is waiting for you to answer a question?

"Yep," I say and then take a sip of tea, hoping he'll get the point that I'm not in a talkative kind of mood.

"Lauren's in advanced art, and she has the lead in the fall play," Mom says. "Don't you, honey?"

Harrison grins. "Advanced art? Is that a real thing?"

I squeeze my fork. "Yes."

"You always liked painting."

Deep, calming breaths.

My parents laugh, again remembering the day he's—once again—referring to. Not that they could forget. Brandon brings it up constantly. I had paint in my hair, on my face, and all over my clothes. Of course, at the time, Dad had been livid with the boys. It's odd how those details are forgotten as time goes on.

The subject of the conversation shifts back to

Harrison, and I try not to gag as I listen to my parents get all gooey over his accomplishments. He graduated high school early and already has his bachelor's degree in architecture. After winning some big award, he was offered a prestigious job position here despite his young age. That's why he's transferring universities to finish up his master's.

Just as we're standing to clear the dishes, my phone goes off in my purse from the next room. I look at Mom, begging her to let me get it.

"I can handle this," Harrison offers as he takes a stack of plates, smiling at my mother in a practiced parent-melting way.

Mom waves me off. "Go on."

I race into the next room just before the call goes to voice mail.

"About time," Riley says.

After bounding up the stairs to my bedroom, I tell my best friend everything.

"Is he cute?" she asks after I finish.

"Well, yes...he's actually pretty hot." I roll my eyes, facing the mirror as I try to wipe the dried paint splotch off my cheek. "But that's not the point."

My reflection scowls at me, and my light blue eyes narrow in irritation. At least the encounter has left a pretty flush over my usually fair skin.

"Okay," Riley says. "So the point is that you have a

totally hot—possibly single—guy living in your guest house who used to tease you because he thought you were cute...and that's...bad?"

"I was *ten*. And he didn't tease me because he thought I was cute. He teased me because he's awful."

"Well," she says, and I can tell from her tone that she's smirking. "You're not ten now."

Just as I'm about to further explain why Harrison is the spawn of evil, there's a knock at the door.

"I gotta go," I say. "Mom's come to grovel."

Riley protests, but I say goodbye and hang up, knowing she'll attack me for more information at school tomorrow.

I swing the door open, ready to whine, but it's not Mom.

Crossing my arms, I glare at Harrison. "What do you want?"

"You don't look happy to see me, Laura-Lou."

I cringe at the nickname. I hated it when my mom used it when I was ten, and I hate it now.

"Please go away," I say.

Harrison's about to respond when his eyes drift behind me to my room, and his jaw goes slack. "Whoa," he mutters. "Did a bottle of glitter explode in there?"

I stand up a little straighter and refuse to answer.

He brushes past me, and I gape at him.

He's in my room.

I don't want him in here.

Harrison picks up knick-knacks to study them, and, one by one, I take them from him and carefully set them back in their places.

"Please don't touch that." I rescue a vase filled with crepe paper flowers from his clutches. "And not that either!"

I try to pull a picture frame out of his grasp, but he's a lot taller than I am, and he holds it above his head while he looks at it.

"Huh," he says.

Irritated, I set my hands on my hips. "Huh, what?"

"Your boyfriend's kind of..."

It's the picture from last year's prom, and Tyler is certainly not my boyfriend. We only went together because Vance Teller asked vile Kally Prath even though he'd flirted with me all semester in first-period language arts. Still, I feel the need to defend Tyler, even if he is a bit of a dweeb.

"Kind of what?" I demand.

Harrison grins and finally hands me the frame. "Nothing."

He continues his perusal of my room, and I tap my foot, waiting for him to get bored and leave. I know if I let myself appear rattled, this will be too much fun for him. Predators are like that.

I must not show fear.

"You're kind of tense." He runs his hand along my sparkling window casing. "Your dad let you do this?"

Actually, Dad was a tiny bit angry.

I give him a bored shrug.

"You're one of the girls who tries everything they see on Pinterest, aren't you?"

At that, I can't keep my mouth shut. I lean forward and narrow my eyes. "I'm one of those girls who designs things that other people try to *copy* off of Pinterest."

He raises an eyebrow, his expression saying, "La-di-da."

We stare at each other for a moment, making our assessments. Harrison's hair is a little darker than it used to be. It's still blond, I think. But there's a lot of brown in it, too. He wears it pretty short, but it's just long enough to be slightly messy.

He does it on purpose, the snarky part of my brain thinks. *He probably uses more hair products than you do.*

It's weird. Harrison's so pretty now. But not in a girly way—in a very manly, could be the swoon-worthy star of a popular teen series kind of way.

It's unsettling.

"All right, Lauren. Here's how this will work," he says suddenly.

Crossing my arms, I stare at him and wait for him to continue.

"I'll stay out of your business," he says. "If you stay out of mine."

I raise an eyebrow. "Why, exactly, would I be interested in getting into your 'business?'"

Harrison laughs and gives me a knowing look. He tosses a sequined pillow back on my bed, disturbing my cat, who's been watching Harrison with suspicious eyes.

Then he strides to me and does the unthinkable—he sets his hands on my shoulders and leans down.

And, much to my horror, my heart stops. It just *stops*. I go cold and then hot, and every square inch of me tingles. Oh, and I hate him. But good heavens, his lips look scrumptious.

He stops about five inches from my face and looks me in the eyes. "I know you had a thing for me when we were young, and you're probably getting yourself all twitterpated at the thought of me living just out back. This could be hard for you, and I want you to know I understand that, and I'll try not to make it any more difficult. But I'm not interested in you in that way, so you'll have to move past it."

I sputter, and my cheeks grow red—not with a pretty girlish flush but in full-out anger.

"I *hated* you," I snarl.

Harrison pats my shoulders in the most condescending way possible. "It's all right. I understand that you're just not mature enough to discuss it without getting defensive."

He gives me a patronizing smile and strides into the hall.

"I didn't...what is wrong with..." I can't even form a coherent thought, and I shake with indignant fury.

"Don't misunderstand me," Harrison says. "I think you're a sweet girl, and if you can manage it, I'd like us to be friendly while I'm here."

With those last words, the door shuts behind him, and I'm left gaping at painted pink and white stripes.

Chapter Two
November 2nd

"Lauren, are you with us?" Mrs. Camberly calls from the auditorium steps.

I glance over, script in hand. I haven't a clue what she just asked me because I've been venting to Riley about how truly awful Harrison is.

"Are you listening?" the teacher asks.

"I'm sorry," I say, shrinking in my seat.

I'm the lead; this is practically my play. I can't shirk like this.

"We're going to go over your first scene."

I nod and leap up.

Tyler plays the part opposite me, and he raises an eyebrow, obviously surprised that I'm off today. We run through our lines, and I try my best to forget Harrison's obnoxious—and probably rehearsed—monologue from yesterday.

As if I ever liked the paint-flinging troll-boy. Please.

After we are finished for the afternoon, Mrs. Camberly runs over our notes. She tells me my heart wasn't in it today.

And she's right. But I'll do better tomorrow.

Once she dismisses us, I pull my backpack on my shoulder and find Riley. Together, we walk to my car. Riley doesn't bother with a coat since she has cheer practice in a few minutes. As soon as we step outside, Riley shivers. I'm sure she's going to freeze.

"Where are you going to film your video now that you can't use the guest house?" she asks, ignoring a gust of cold, autumn wind.

I shake my head and groan. "I don't know. I guess I'll do it in my room."

"I can help after cheer."

"That would be nice," I say, and then I stop and really look at her. She has a guilty expression on her face. "You just want to see Harrison."

My friend shrugs as she rubs her bare arms. "I'm a little curious."

"Fine." I roll my eyes and get in my car. "Whatever."

"What's your mom making for dinner?" she asks as she continues to shiver in the school parking lot.

Cranking up the heat, I say, "I don't know, but she won't care if you stay."

Riley grins. I pull the door shut, and she races back to the building, waving over her shoulder.

Try as I might, I can't think of anywhere I have an excuse to be, so I head home. As I pull around the back, I see Harrison's truck is gone. Good. I walk into the house, happy I won't have to deal with him.

When I shut the front door, Mom calls from the back, "Lauren?"

"Yeah, it's me."

After tossing my backpack on the couch, I make my way into the kitchen to her. It's the first chance we've had to talk since last night.

She eyes me, her expression wary.

"Why didn't you tell me?" I ask.

The stove timer goes off, and she pulls a loaf of homemade bread out of the oven. Normally she just uses the bread machine, so, clearly, she's showing off.

"Lauren," she sighs. "You're always so dramatic. I had been meaning to tell you, but then Harrison got here a few days early..."

"How hard is it to give me some warning?" I pause. "I'm not dramatic."

She raises an eyebrow, and I shrug.

The aroma of freshly baked bread makes me hungry, and I open the pantry to rummage through its contents.

"Brandon's going to be home in a few weeks

anyway," Mom says. "The boys will be so busy catching up with old friends, I'm sure they'll leave you alone."

They'll leave me alone all right. Because I'm an embarrassing lovesick puppy who's apparently been pining away for Harrison for the last eight years.

I slice an apple with more force than necessary and slather it with peanut butter. With my snack in hand, I walk out of the kitchen. "I have to work on the video for my blog."

"Dinner's at six," Mom calls.

I turn back. "Riley's going to stop by. Is that all right?"

Mom's busy chopping vegetables with her fancy crinkle cutter. "Sure."

I nod and jog up the steps.

"So you're going to be an architect?" Riley's eyelashes flutter.

Harrison smiles, obviously enjoying my pretty cheerleader friend's attention. "That's right."

Riley twirls her blond braid between her fingers, smitten.

Honestly.

It's not like he's studying to be a neurosurgeon or a biophysicist. He'll design apartment complexes and community centers. Big deal.

16

"I think that's amazing," Riley coos.

We've finished dinner, and now we're in the living room, drinking coffee. Well, my parents, Harrison, and Riley are drinking coffee.

I dunk my tea bag demurely in my mug and then set it on the saucer.

"How's your tea, Lady Laura-Lou?" Harrison teases.

I glance at him and give him a bored look of disdain. "Just lovely, thank you for asking."

For someone who says he's going to stay out of my way, he's still as obnoxious as ever.

His mouth twitches. "You can have coffee when you grow up."

"You can have tea when you..." The retort dies on my lips when I realize I have absolutely nothing to say.

"Learn some manners?" Harrison supplies.

Grudgingly, I have to admit that would have been a pretty good comeback.

Harrison leans forward, daring me to keep up the banter. My eyes flicker to his biceps, which are muscular under his almost-tight T-shirt. Once I realize where my attention has drifted, I rip my gaze back to his face.

Why did Harrison, of all people, have to grow up to be so devastatingly good looking? It's such a shame.

It's such a waste.

"Why does Harrison call you Laura-Lou?" Riley asks me, her nose wrinkling as she says it.

"Everyone called her Laura-Lou when she was young." He turns to my parents "Didn't they?"

Mom laughs, nodding, and she and Dad launch into an embarrassing story from my youth. Ignoring them, I sip my tea and browse through my phone like I'm very important and can't be bothered with this trivial conversation.

Unfortunately, I have no emails and no messages. Nothing.

When I glance up, I find Riley studying me.

"Are you ready to help me?" I ask her.

Riley glances at Harrison, and her expression morphs to wistful. She obviously has no desire to leave him.

She'll have to get over it.

I grab her arm and yank her up. "Say goodnight, Riley."

She giggles and gives Harrison this little nose scrunch that the boys at school can't seem to resist. Voice just on the side of breathy, she says, "It was *very* nice to meet you."

Harrison raises his eyebrows at me and then winks at her. "Nice to meet you too, Riley."

Gag. Gag. Gag.

"Okay, we're done here," I say as I pull her along.

Once we're safely in my room and the door is shut, she turns to me and gapes. "He's *gorgeous.*"

"Yes, I'm aware of that."

She shakes her head as if I don't understand. "No, I mean he's just...so...yummy."

Already getting a headache, I rub my temples. "Can we focus?"

"Can I have him?"

"What?" I look up sharply. "No."

Her face falls. "I thought you didn't want him."

I resist the urge to roll my eyes. "I don't want him."

"So why can't I have him?" she demands.

"Why are we doing this?" I ask. "We're supposed to be working on the video."

"I'm taking that as a 'Yes, Riley, of course, you can have him.'"

"Would you drop it?" I snap.

Ignoring me completely, she does a little happy dance and finally takes my phone.

"What are you making today?" she asks.

"We're spray painting the tips of these feathers, dipping the ends in glitter, and then making a wreath."

Riley eyes the white feathers with confusion. "Festive."

"It will be, see?" I show her the finished project, which is also decorated with sprigs of holly and berries.

She shrugs. Riley's not really the crafty type.

"Do your parents care that you're spray painting in your room?" she asks.

"I've already done the actual painting."

In the garage. The cold, smelly garage.

I've gathered the supplies, and Riley starts the video. It's going well, and I'm halfway through when Penelope, my cat, jumps directly in the middle of the project, sending feathers everywhere.

I shriek, which scares Penelope, and then she scrambles off the table. As she's jumping down, her hind foot kicks the aluminum pie plate of glitter, and it flies into the air, dousing me in gold sparkles.

Riley's squeals join mine as she leaps away from the mess. The cat tears about the room, terrified. Two seconds later, my door flies open.

"What in the world—" Dad says, and then his eyes go wide.

Penelope rushes into the hall, a blur of white and gold glittery fur.

"Not in your room!" Mom cries. "Lauren!"

I tip my head back and try to shake the glitter out of my hair so none will fall in my eyes (which hurts, let me tell you), and then I look at Mom. "Where did you expect me to do it?"

"Watch your tone, young lady," Dad says, crossing his arms.

I almost—almost—lose it, but he's right. I'm not

an angst-riddled teen. I'm a good girl who gets good grades and doesn't talk back to her parents. Not very often, anyway.

Mom has her hand over her eyes as if she can't bear to witness the mess. "Go brush off in the backyard. Then you'll have to vacuum everything."

"I think I'm going to go," Riley whispers.

She makes a quick exit, and I follow her down the stairs.

"And, Lauren," Dad hollers down. "Get the glitter off the cat!"

It's freezing outside, and it's started to snow. I shiver as I attempt to shake myself free of glitter.

"What happened to you?" Harrison asks from behind me.

I refuse to turn. "Don't you have poor people on the Internet to harass? You seem like the type who would enjoy that."

"Feisty," he mutters, and then he swipes his hand over my shoulders.

I flinch away from him.

"Would you just relax?" Harrison says, and then he steps closer. With a firmer hand, he begins brushing the glitter off. His hand drifts down my shoulder blades to my lower back.

My pulse jumps (out of anger, I'm sure), and I step away. "Watch your hands."

Harrison snorts. "Like I'd want to go there."

"I've got this." I motion him away. "You can scamper off now."

I look back at my cardigan, which is not coming clean. On the ground, gold glitter twinkles over the snow, lit by the dim glow of the porch light.

A breeze blows through the yard, and I shiver.

"You're going to freeze out here without a coat," Harrison says.

I just keep brushing.

Harrison rocks on his heels. "Come in the guest house. The tile's easy to clean up."

Another violent shiver runs through me. "Fine."

I follow him in. Once I'm through the doorway, I gape at the space—my space. There are auto magazines on the kitchenette counter, and a suitcase of clothes spills over on the couch. It looks like a boy lives here. A messy boy.

But it's warmer than outside.

As soon as we're in, I pull off my cardigan. When I toss it onto the tile and look back at Harrison, his eyes dart away. A strange flutter travels through my stomach, and I smooth imaginary wrinkles on my tank-top.

"You still have some..." Harrison steps forward, his

hand hovering over my head.

When I don't flinch away, he runs his fingers through my hair and fluffs it out. Sparkles fall, surrounding us both.

Trying to hide a gulp, I say, "You're getting it on your shirt."

"No," he says, and our eyes meet. "*You're* getting it on my shirt."

I don't like him. He's a jerk. He made my summers miserable.

So why am I running my hand along his arm, wiping away glitter? Why are my fingertips brushing his chest while I pretend it's not because I want to touch him?

Harrison's eyes darken, and he whispers, "Lauren, what are you doing?"

Suddenly, my imagination runs wild. His hands are still in my hair. What if his fingers were to shift, no longer shaking glitter free, but wrapping in the strands...?

What if he gently tugged me closer, leaned in...?

"Lauren?"

I blink at him, jerk my hands from his chest, and then swat him away from my hair.

Get a grip, Lauren.

"What?" I ask.

Harrison gives me a weird look, and then he

shoves his hands in his pockets.

"Um, thanks," I say as I swipe my cardigan off the floor, give it one more hearty shake, and walk to the door. "I'm sure that's most of it."

"You still look like a casualty of a glitter factory mishap."

I'm feeling all fluttery and off. "Whatever."

Harrison frowns at me and shrugs out of his jacket. "It's too cold without a coat."

"It's only about fifty feet to the house."

"Still."

He tosses me the jacket. I try not to think about how warm it is as I pull it on and escape through the door.

Chapter Three
November 16th

I pretend to read a book, adjust my fake eyeglass frames, and then look startled when Tyler enters from stage right. He smiles. I smile. And we continue our lines.

The huge stage lights shift as our tech crew adjusts them, and I try to ignore the distracting changes.

It's three days until opening night, and we've started our late-night rehearsals. Lines are memorized, and we're finally working with the set. The auditorium smells like paint, dusty costumes, and the starch used to tighten fabric flats.

I love it. Theater is what I will miss about high school the most.

Tyler and I finish our scene, and then we go down to the auditorium while the other actors run their lines. I take off my fake glasses and twirl them in my hand as I scoot into an aisle and take a place next to Riley. Tyler finds the spot in front of us, pushes the seat down with his knees, and drapes his arm over the back of the chair.

"That was really good," Riley says.

I tap my heeled boot on the tan cement floor. "I stumbled over that last line."

Tyler rolls his eyes. "Barely. No one noticed."

"I didn't notice," Riley agrees.

The dark blue curtains close as the first act finishes. With a scurry of movement onstage, the tech crew works to quickly change sets.

Hopefully, they'll get better at it before Thursday. It's taking an awfully long time.

Someone hollers for Mrs. Camberly, and the curtains slide open. A few guys in the tech crew ask our theater teacher questions about placement.

Tyler and Riley discuss their plans for Christmas break, but my attention, however, is on the stage.

"Is that Grant?" I ask, disbelief lacing my voice.

Riley looks up. "Oh, yeah. Coach told him he can't do basketball if he doesn't get his grade up in his theater theory class, so he's doing some extra credit for Mrs. Camberly."

Mr. All-Star High School Golden Boy is helping with the tech crew? There's so much wrong with that.

I glance at Riley. I guess if a cheerleader can

coexist in this world, Grant can too.

Tyler snorts. "Who fails theater theory? That's the easiest class. It's filled with freshman."

"Why did he even take it to begin with?" I ask Riley.

She shrugs. Friendly with nearly everyone, she knows most of the school's gossip, but she doesn't know everything.

They apparently get the set in place because the crew disappears into the back. Mrs. Camberly calls for us to begin again. I'm not in the beginning of the second act, but Tyler is, so he hurries to the stage.

Looking out of place and more than a little uncomfortable, Grant emerges from the side door and jogs down the auditorium steps.

"Grant!" Riley waves him over.

Grant spots her, looks relieved to see someone from his usual crowd, and walks to us.

"Hey, Riley," he says as he takes the seat that Tyler just vacated. Then his eyes drift to me. "Lauren."

There's a little flutter in my stomach like there always is when Grant talks to me—which isn't often because our classes don't usually overlap, and we don't exactly have the same extracurricular activities.

He runs a hand through his blond hair, still looking a little uncomfortable to be in the auditorium at nearly nine o'clock at night instead of in the afternoon for an assembly.

In fact, I doubt he's been in here for anything other than an assembly. Even the theater theory class is held in a classroom in the hall with the other electives.

"So you got roped into tech duty?" I ask.

He nods, and a crooked smile tilts his lips. "Are the tech guys always that...?"

"Weird?" I supply.

Grant laughs. "Yeah."

Riley nods. "Yes, but you get used to them."

One of the guys in question yells some intergalactic movie quote backstage. He's so loud, it echoes through the entire auditorium. Mrs. Camberly purses her lips, jogs up the stairs, and disappears behind the curtains.

Riley rolls her eyes. "Maybe."

After a few moments, Mrs. Camberly emerges and calls for the actors in the library scene to come forward. Riley bounds off to join the others. She's elated because she actually has a line this time.

"So, this is kind of your thing, huh?" Grant asks, looking around.

I shift, a little nervous. "One of them anyway."

"Yeah?" He turns behind him to make sure that Mrs. Camberly is occupied, and then he hops over the back of his seat and settles next to me.

I've never seen anyone do it with quite that much

grace. All of the guys have jumped over the auditorium chairs at one point, but the uncoordinated types that seem to be drawn to theater usually fall on their faces.

"What else?" Grant asks.

He's right next to me, looking at me. I blink at him. "What else, what?"

A smile spreads across his face. "You said theater is just 'one of your things.' What else do you do?"

"Oh." My eyes drop, and I smooth my gray knee-length skirt. "I like to make things."

Which isn't entirely true. I prefer to embellish things, but I'm sure this handsome jock doesn't really care.

"What do you make?" he asks.

Grant's just being nice because out of everyone in this room, I'm the lesser evil at the moment. My friendship with Riley has kept me from the complete social death that's usually the result of being in theater.

"Crafty things mostly," I say. "But I can paint a little, sketch a little."

"That's cool."

I nod, unsure what else to say.

We both watch Mrs. Camberly give instructions to the group onstage. After that, our teacher calls it a night, and we gather for our notes.

Finally, we're dismissed. It's almost ten, and I'm exhausted. I find my jacket and purse, and I then hunt

Riley down. She's a social butterfly, and she'll likely talk for another fifteen minutes before I can drag her away. It was her turn to drive tonight, though, so I have to wait.

I eventually find her standing in a small group, and Grant is with her. A couple of sophomores step aside to make the circle larger as I join them.

"Did you drive, Lauren?" Grant asks.

"No, I rode with Riley."

Grant tosses his keys in his hand. "I can drive you home."

A stunned and very obvious silence descends over the circle.

"Oh," I say, just as bewildered as the rest of the group. "I mean, Riley—"

"It's fine," Riley interrupts and gives me a very pointed look. "I'm going to be a few more minutes anyway. You guys should go."

My stomach tightens, and my nerves threaten to turn me into a babbling mess.

"Okay," I squeak.

Grant tosses his keys again. "You have all your stuff?"

I nod quickly before I realize I look like a bobblehead doll and abruptly stop. The underclassmen around us look on me with awe.

Grant, the beloved, handsome star of everything

is driving me home.

We walk out of the auditorium side by side, and just before we're through the doorway, I look over my shoulder at Riley. She meets my eyes and does a twirly, happy cheer right there in the main left-hand aisle.

I attempt to smile in a way that doesn't make me look seasick and follow Grant to his car. Clouds have stretched over the sky, and the school lights seem to reflect off of them. Sporadic snowflakes drift to the ground, and it's very cold.

When we get to Grant's car, he has to shove assorted sports gear over so I'll have a place to sit. It might be my imagination, but he seems a little nervous.

I know why I'm nervous around him, but why would he be nervous around me?

After my seat is clear, I crawl in, and he shuts the door for me. The leather upholstery is freezing, and I shiver.

"It will warm up in a minute," Grant assures me as he starts the engine and fiddles with the thermostat.

There are various tacky decals in the back window, and assignments spill out of the backpack at my feet. Even though the car isn't brand new, it's not too old either.

"I live in the Pine Grove subdivision," I tell him.

"I know."

When I give Grant a funny look, he rubs the back of his neck. "Jordan Cooper lives over there, and I've seen you around."

A pleasant warmth spreads in my chest. He's noticed me?

I adjust my scarf, straightening the already perfect knot. "I'm only a few houses down from him."

After we've driven for a few minutes, the air loses its chill. Grant cranks up the fan, and I stretch my boot-encased toes toward the warmth.

"Why did you take theater theory?" I ask, trying to chase away the awkward silence.

Grant looks over and gives me a wry smile. "I wanted an easy A."

I bite my lip, trying not to smile. Theater theory is an easy A.

"So what happened?" I ask.

He grimaces and turns onto the highway. "*Oedipus Rex* happened."

I groan. "It's awful, isn't it?"

"And then we read through *The Importance of Being Earnest.*"

"Oh, no." I shake my head vigorously and laugh. "That one is wonderful! It was my favorite in the class."

Grant laughs with me. "Well, I failed both tests."

How do you fail one of Mrs. Camberly's tests? Half of the questions are multiple choice and the rest are true or false. Sometimes she'll put in an optional essay question at the end, but those are just for extra credit.

"So how did you get roped into tech duty?" I ask.

"Mrs. Camberly said she was short a few hands, so, knowing I was failing, Coach Smith generously volunteered me."

"Is it awful?"

He glances at me and gives me a smile that I've seen directed at the school's elite before. "It has its perks."

My stomach flip-flops, and I'm glad it's dark because my cheeks are hot.

"My house is the one with the porch lights on," I say as Grant takes the last turn.

A lot of the houses in our area are newer, built in subdivisions that have sprouted up in the last fifteen years. But our neighborhood is old and has character. The houses are large and have picture windows and landscaped yards. The lots are big, and because of it, many have small guest houses or even pools in the back.

I've lived here my entire life, and I can't imagine living anywhere else. Of course, I'll have to get over that. I can't stay with my parents forever.

As a little girl, I imagined I'd have a Prince Charming at this point in my life—a nice boyfriend who would take me to movies and all the school dances. A few years later, after college, we would get married, adopt two springer spaniel puppies, and move into a house just like the one Grant's pulling into right now.

My younger self would be very disappointed in me.

I unbuckle my seat belt as soon as the car stops. Grant seems unsure whether he should turn the engine off or keep it running.

I make the decision for him by jumping out and giving him a quick wave. "Thanks again for the ride."

Grant smiles and nods. "Anytime."

After an awkward moment, I jog up the garden-light-lined steps to the front door. Movement in the window catches my eye, and as soon as I reach for my keys, the door opens.

"That's not Riley's car." Dad narrows his eyes at Grant's taillights. "Who drove you home?"

Oh, bad words. I didn't even think to call them and ask.

"Grant," I supply, still standing on the freezing front step.

Dad ushers me inside. "Who's Grant?"

"He's a guy from school."

Obviously, right?

"Is he in theater?" Mom asks, joining Dad. "Do we

know him?"

I bob on my toes. "No, he's more into sports and stuff."

"What was he doing driving you home?" Dad asks. "Are you dating him? You know the rules. We meet the guys you go out with first."

Groaning on the inside, I follow them into the living room off the foyer.

"It's really not a big deal..." I trail off when my eyes land on Harrison, who's sitting on the couch with one of Dad's outdoor magazines forgotten on his lap.

Harrison raises his eyebrows, and his eyes light with humor, obviously enjoying seeing me in trouble. "Hey, Laura-Lou."

I grit my teeth, ignore him, and turn back to my parents. "I promise we're not dating—we're not anything. He was just being nice. And I should have called. I messed up, and I'm sorry."

My parents exchange a look, and then the tension eases from Dad's posture.

Sometimes being the baby of the family can be a real pain. I don't remember Brandon being saddled with this many rules. Or maybe it's because I'm a girl. Whatever it is—it's annoying.

"Call us next time," Mom says, and then she goes back to the couch and picks up her discarded novel.

The remnants of a batch of popcorn sit in a bowl

on the coffee table. Half-full coffee cups join it. It all looks very cozy in here. I glance again at Harrison and frown.

As if he can read my thoughts, he smirks at me. The look makes me want to kick his feet off the coffee table. I might too, but his casual brown oxfords are actually very nice, and they don't deserve my wrath.

"I'm going to bed," I say and turn from the room. "Night."

"We'll be up shortly," Mom says, but she's already engrossed in her book again.

As I walk into my room, a text comes through on my phone. I dig it out of my purse.

Are you home? Was it awesome? Did Grant kiss you???

I smile at Riley's enthusiasm as I write her back. *Yes. Kinda. No!*

As soon as it goes through, Riley calls.

"What do you mean 'kinda?'" she demands.

I unwind my scarf from my neck and hang it on the organizer in my closet. "I don't know. It was a little uncomfortable."

"Good uncomfortable?"

My jewelry box is a mess of necklaces I rarely wear and dozens of pairs of earrings. I take out the pearl earrings I was wearing tonight and set them on top.

"Good uncomfortable, I guess."

Her exasperation radiates through the phone. "Don't you like him? During our freshman year you swooned every time he passed you in the hall."

I've always kind of liked Grant, but over the years, I wonder if watching him from afar has finally lost some of its appeal. And last year I gave up on Grant and my affections shifted to Jason Teller. For all the good that did me.

But there was definitely something between us tonight.

"Sure," I say slowly. "I still kind of like him."

Riley laughs. "You're so fickle."

I might be. I can't argue that when my mind keeps drifting to the loathsome creature who's downstairs, sitting on the couch, drinking my mother's coffee, and reading my father's magazines.

"Get some sleep," she says. "You sound listless." Then, before we hang up for the night, she reminds me, "I have an FBLA thing tomorrow morning, so don't pick me up."

I tell her I remember and finally get her off the phone. After I wash off my makeup and change out of my school clothes, I crawl into bed. Even though I'm exhausted, I can't shut my mind off, and I end up staring at the ceiling.

My mom peeks in the room about an hour later and whispers goodnight when she sees I'm not asleep.

The house goes dark, and finally, well after midnight, I drift off.

Instead of waking to my alarm, I'm startled by Dad knocking on my already open door.

"Hey, kiddo," he says while I blink in the dark room.

The only light comes from the hall, and I look at my clock. It reads five-ten, which is twenty minutes before my alarm should go off.

"It snowed last night, so you'll need to give yourself a little extra time," he continues.

I groan, wanting more than anything to go back to sleep.

"Okay," I croak out.

"I'm on my way out," Dad says. "And Mom has to leave early this morning. Will you be all right getting out by yourself?"

"I'll be fine."

He says goodbye, and I pull myself out of bed. Mom leaves, and the house is oddly quiet. Even Penelope's absent. She usually sleeps on my pillow, but she still hasn't forgiven me for holding her down and brushing the glitter out of her fur.

Since the snow is heavy this morning, I opt for a pair of jeans and my cute faux fur-trimmed snow boots. After a quick breakfast, I pull on a heavy coat and trudge out to my car.

It's already snowed several inches, and it doesn't look like it's going to slow down anytime soon. As I scoot into my seat to start the car, snow falls on me from the roof and slides down the back of my neck.

Shivering violently, I turn the key, but nothing happens.

I try again.

Still nothing.

Oh, no.

Dad's already at work, and Mom has a meeting this morning. Riley's already at school.

I could call Grandpa, but he and Grandma live all the way across town, and I don't want to wake them this early or have him drive through the snow to get here.

I try the car one more time, just to be sure.

It's not going to start.

With no other option, I trudge through the snow to the back.

Wishing with all my being I didn't have to do this, I knock on the guest house door.

Chapter Four
November 17th

There are no lights on in the guest house, and I don't hear anything after I knock. I know Harrison is home because his truck is parked right here in the circular drive.

Growling under my breath, I take off my glove and knock louder this time, hoping Harrison will hear it now that fabric isn't muffling the sound.

After a few moments, a light flicks on in the main room. I hold my breath and hope that Harrison isn't one of those grumpy morning people.

The door opens, and Harrison stands on the other side, looking sleep-rumpled in his pajama pants.

And only pajama pants.

I gape at him. Then, trying not to stare, I yank my eyes up to his face.

He's still too asleep to notice.

"Lauren?" He runs a hand through his hair. "What's wrong? What time is it?"

Freezing despite my heavy coat, I cross my arms. "My car won't start, and I have to get to school. Do you think you can...fix it...or something?"

He squints at me, rubs his hands over his face, and then waves me inside.

It's so warm. My cheeks begin to tingle as soon as I walk through the door. I pull off my gloves and set them aside so I can rub feeling back into my frozen fingers.

"I'll be right back." Harrison still sounds groggy as he steps into the back bedroom.

Shifting from one foot to the other, I scan the room. It's more orderly than it was the last time I was in here, but it still has a different feel. A very Harrison feel. It's sort of suffocating.

In just a few minutes, Harrison steps out of the bedroom looking a lot more awake than he did when he first answered the door.

He grabs a coat and a pair of keys. "Stay here."

I'm about to remind him that he'll need my keys to check the car, but he's already out the door.

He'll figure it out soon enough.

Then I hear the rumble of his truck starting. I frown at the door.

"How late are you?" he asks when he comes in.

41

There's snow in his hair and on his coat, and little flakes fall to the floor as he walks through the room.

"I'm not yet," I answer as I watch the snow melt on the tile. "I got up early since it snowed."

He disappears back into the bedroom, and I wait, feeling the clock ticking.

"Don't you need my keys to check my car?" I call back to him.

"No," he hollers back. "I'll just drive you, and then I can look at your car later."

A coil of nerves knots itself in my stomach. It's too early for this.

He comes back out, looking ready for the day. His hair is perfect—now just mildly disheveled—and he's shaved.

"Let's go." He opens the door.

I hesitate. "You don't have to drive me…"

"How else are you going to get there?"

I don't know. It just doesn't seem like going with Harrison is a very good idea.

Finally, I relent and walk out the door. The sky is just lightening above the thick, gray clouds.

Harrison holds my door open for me. It's obviously too early for him to remember that he's a jerk.

I mumble a thank you as I climb in. Since he started it early, the truck is delightfully warm. He slides into the driver's seat, fiddles with the heater controls, and then pulls around the drive.

It's as if the middle console doesn't exist. It feels as if he's *right there*. I can even smell the faint scent of his aftershave or deodorant or whatever it is that he put on this morning.

"Sorry to wake you up." I look out the window at the white landscape.

I can feel him glance my way. "It's all right. I had to be up soon anyway."

That's right. He started at the architectural firm yesterday.

"How do you like the job?" I ask just so I'll have something to say.

Out of the corner of my eye, I see him shrug. "So far all I've done is fill out paperwork and go through training."

It suddenly hits me that Harrison's an actual adult. He'll be finishing up college soon. He has a job—a real job with a retirement plan and investment opportunities.

And here I am, a little girl asking him to drive me to school.

I shift in my seat, feeling even more uncomfortable than I was before.

"What is it?" he asks.

Surprised he's perceptive enough to pick up on

my discomfort, I look over at him. "Nothing."

He grins wide, an ornery expression spreading over his face. "Whatever, Laura-Lou. You have that prim and proper look you get when you don't like something."

"Stop calling me that."

Harrison shakes his head. "That's probably not going to happen."

I clench my hands in my lap. Despite his chivalrous, "to-the-rescue" attitude this morning, he's still a loathsome toad.

A hot toad, mind you. But a toad nonetheless.

We finally reach the school, and I quickly hop out of his truck. "Thanks for driving me."

A few of the girls nearby stop and stare, their eyes wide as they gape at Harrison.

"Hey, Lauren?" Harrison calls as I begin to shut the door.

Irritated, I stick my head back in the cab. "What?"

"I know you're still hung up on me, but next time let's not fake car trouble so I'll give you a ride. It's a little over the top, don't you think?"

I practically shake with anger, but when I try to think of a retort, I can only sputter.

He has the audacity to grin at me before he puts his truck back in gear. Growling, I slam the door. Even through the layer of metal, I can hear his answering laugh.

I turn on my heel. Feeling his eyes on me, I hold my head high as I stomp through the snow and stride into the school.

There is nothing cute about the garage. The walls are white, but they aren't even painted. It's a drywall white with putty and tape marks.

Dad remodeled it a few years back, and though it's a lot roomier than it was, he definitely didn't put any thought into design.

Honestly, why would he? It's a garage.

And I'm stuck with it until Harrison moves out.

I'm standing on a barstool I've dragged from the kitchen, and I'm attempting to hang a huge piece of pink and white canvas. I have it stretched over a tall metal cabinet, and I'm trying to hold it in place with paint cans at the top.

It's not going well.

The right side slips just as I'm scooting the can in place over the left corner, and I growl in frustration as the piece yanks away completely and crumples to the floor.

"What exactly are you trying to accomplish?"

Still teetering perilously on top of the barstool, I squeeze my eyes shut and try to trap in a few very unladylike words.

"Shouldn't you be at work?" I ask Harrison as I crawl down.

"Shouldn't you be doing that in something other than high heels?"

I glance at my shoes. They aren't high heels at all; they're kitten heels.

He eyes my rickety setup. "And why don't you use a ladder instead of a swiveling kitchen chair?"

Originally, I had planned to use the ladder. Until I got out here and realized that Dad has anchored them all to the top of the back wall where they'll be out of the way. Now they're just high enough I can't reach them.

Irritated, I point to the ladders.

Harrison laughs, obviously enjoying my dilemma.

When he sees the murderous expression on my face, he says, "Your Dad has pegboard over there. I can hang it for you if you have some clothespins."

I tap my foot. This morning when I asked for help, I ended up regretting it.

He crosses his arms, still looking at the peg board. "You probably don't have clothespins, though. We could use clamps—where are you going?"

Don't have clothespins. *Please.*

When I return, I hold out a fistful in my hand, rather proud of myself.

Harrison looks at them, raises an eyebrow, and then meets my eyes. "You've dipped them in *glitter.*"

They were for a birthday banner post last year, and they were spectacular. He wouldn't scoff if he knew how many visitors my blog has gotten since I added it.

No, he probably would.

"Will the glitter hinder their performance?" I ask. "Are they in any way unusable?"

Harrison shakes his head and snatches the clothespins out of my hand. His obnoxious smile tips his lips again. "I forgot how much fun you are, Lauren."

And—oh my—butterflies erupt in my stomach when he says my name. Not "Laura-Lou" or some other equally cute and obnoxious nickname—but my actual given name.

No. Not butterflies.

Because I do not like him.

I tamp the feeling down and lock it away so it won't escape again.

"How high does it need to be?" Harrison asks as he picks up a corner of the fabric.

"A little higher," I say, distracted as his shirt rises over his stomach.

He stretches higher, and his shirt shifts a little more. "Like this?"

Bad Lauren.

I rub a spot behind my ear, feeling a little guilty.

47

"Maybe just a little higher..."

Oh, I give up. I can look at him, can't I? I can detest someone while admiring their hotness?

Suddenly he looks over his shoulder, and my eyes snap up to his. Unlike this morning, he definitely notices.

He raises an eyebrow, a knowing look in his eyes. I'm waiting for him to come up with something snarky, but, instead, he says, "How about here?"

"That's fine," I say primly, pretending I wasn't just checking out his abs.

"All right," he answers, pretending he didn't just catch me checking out his abs.

But he knows.

And suddenly, and for no explicable reason, the garage feels rather warm.

Harrison attaches the fabric to the pegs using the clothespins to secure it into place. The fabric is so heavy, I figure it's just going to drag it down like it did about a million times with the paint cans, but it stays in place.

I roll my eyes at his back.

He finishes and turns to face me. "So what was the purpose of this? Just felt the garage needed a little pink?"

"No."

"It's kind of your mission, isn't it? To glitter, paint,

or decoupage the world?"

He's obviously enjoying himself, and I shouldn't rise to his bait...but it's so hard.

I set my hands on my hips. "I do not decoupage."

And it's true. It's not my thing at all.

He rests a hip against the workbench. "No, your preferred medium is glitter. Tell me, does your cat still sparkle?"

I want to tell him that today's project doesn't have a thing to do with glitter, but I'm afraid if I admit I have a craft blog, he'll use it later as ammunition.

Again, Harrison points to the backdrop. "Really, what are you doing with this?"

What excuse am I going to give him for the giant sheet of canvas pinned to the garage wall?

I turn, collect my supplies, and mumble, "I'm-doing-a-video-for-my-blog."

"I didn't catch that."

I turn back around with a tiny, fake Christmas tree in my hand. "I said, I'm doing a video for my blog."

For a moment, it looks like he's digesting that information. I expect him to come up with a quick retort, but he motions to the tree. "And what are you doing with that?"

"I'm using it to hang the finished miniature ornaments I'm making."

"Huh."

That's it. "Huh."

What am I even supposed to do with that?

Trying my best to ignore him, I pull over the card table I found in the coat closet. I flip it on its top and fight to lock the first leg in place. Without a word, Harrison helps.

After we have all the legs extended, he turns it right side up. "Where do you want it?"

"In front of the backdrop."

I fuss with the tablecloth I've picked out and line up my supplies, pretending he's not standing there, still watching.

"Are you good now?" he asks.

"Yep." I can't meet his eyes.

He hovers for a few moments longer, and then he leaves. I adjust my phone on the new tripod that I ordered after the cat/glitter fiasco, and when I'm sure I have it right, I begin.

Terrified Harrison's going to come back while I'm filming, I'm a little tense. Thankfully, I finish without any incidents, and just in time, too. As I'm packing everything up, Harrison walks back in.

"It was just your battery," he says.

Distracted, I look up. "What was?"

"Your car. I jumped it, and it started fine. It looks like the passenger door wasn't completely shut, and the light stayed on."

I stare at him blankly. "You fixed my car?"

He slides his hands into his jeans pockets. "You should probably drive it around a little, let the alternator charge the battery up again."

"Um...okay."

"Are you done in here?" he asks. "Do you want help taking that down?"

I glance at the canvas. "No, I'll leave it for now. I'll need it again in a few days.

Harrison nods. "I left your car running, so you'll probably want to drive around the neighborhood a few times." He looks a little uncomfortable. "Or I can hook it to a battery charger..."

The clock on the wall says it's almost five.

"I need to get to practice anyway."

He nods and wanders the garage. As I'm picking up the last of my stuff, he stops in front of Mom's seed starting station.

Harrison taps one of the long fluorescent lights. "What's this?"

"Mom grows flats of plants from seed every spring," I explain. "She's kind of obsessed."

He looks at the cart. "What does she grow?"

I join him. "Tomatoes, peppers, broccoli, cauliflower, parsley, daisies, basil..."

"Why daisies?" he interrupts.

Surprised, I glance at him.

"Everything you mentioned is edible," he explains. "Why does she grow daisies?"

"She grows a lot of flowers. Those were just the first to pop into my mind."

"Hmmm."

What's with him and those one-word, cryptic responses?

"Your car's running," he reminds me.

I jump, gather all my things in my arms, and walk to the door. Just before I go through, I turn back. "Thanks for fixing my car. And helping with the canvas."

He only nods, but there's something warm and real hidden in his eyes.

As I go into the house, those stupid butterflies escape their cage.

Chapter Five
November 19th

It's opening night, and I have to be to the school by five thirty. There's no time to eat dinner with my parents. Since I'm on my own, I go for my usual apple and peanut butter to get me by. I'm so nervous; I couldn't eat much more anyway.

As I stand here, running my lines through my head, eating my apple, Harrison pulls around the circular drive and parks next to the guest house.

So far this week, he's gone in early every day and gotten off by five. Not that I'm paying attention.

From the safety of the house, I'm able to study Harrison. He's in a suit, but he's already taken off his tie. He swings it in his hand as he unlocks the door.

I lean my elbows on the counter, take another bite of the apple, and continue my perusal. His hair is in its usual carefully executed messy style, but it looks a little softer. Like maybe he's had a rough afternoon, and he's been running his hands through it.

The front door slams, and I jump up, feeling guilty for no reason.

"Lauren?" Mom calls.

"In here."

Mom walks into the kitchen, her arms laden with grocery bags. I jump forward to help, and, together, we dump them on the counter.

After tossing the apple core in the trash, I rummage through the bags.

"When do you have to leave?" Mom asks.

"Five thirty."

Mom looks at her watch and frowns. "Did you eat dinner?"

When I tell her what I ate, she rolls her eyes and pulls out several bags of deli lunch meat. "I'll make you a sandwich."

My stomach lurches at the thought.

"I'm good, Mom."

She hesitates, looking unsure whether sending me out the door without a proper meal would make her an unfit mother.

"I have to go now anyway," I tell her as I fill my water bottle. "I'll see you after the show."

"Break a leg."

I rush out of the kitchen, grab my costumes from

my room, and then hurry to my car. It wasn't as cold today, but now that the sun's set, it's getting pretty chilly.

Just as I'm sliding into the driver's seat, I get a text from Grant.

Can I drive you tonight?

Immediately, my eyes dart to the guest house. Then, shaking my head, I write back, *Can you be here soon?*

My phone rings, and I answer it.

"I'm just leaving Jordan's," Grant says. "I'll be there in a minute."

Immediately, I run into the house. Out of breath, I burst into the kitchen.

"Can Grant drive me tonight?" I ask, and then I step back because Harrison's now standing there with my mom.

Mom looks over, surprised to see me back. She scoops up a pile of sliced carrots, tosses them into a skillet, and then she says, "I suppose...if we meet him first."

Harrison leans on the counter, watching me.

Uncomfortable, I look back at Mom. "I'm running kind of late..."

"No," she says without hesitation. "If I don't meet him, you don't ride with him."

Knowing it's an argument I won't win, I just nod

and go wait in the foyer. Harrison's footsteps echo in the room behind me. I don't have to turn to know it's him. I can feel it.

"How's your car running?"

I look over my shoulder. "Oh, it's been fine since you fixed it. Thanks again."

He leans against the wall, eating a carrot stick. "Sure."

I raise my eyebrows slightly, trying to mentally tell him to go away. I don't need him hovering when I answer the door.

He raises his eyebrows in return, telling me he's enjoying standing right there.

Sighing, I look away. A car door shuts outside, and I practically leap to the door.

"You look desperate," Harrison says. "Bad idea."

I glare at him over my shoulder.

He shrugs. "Trying to help."

Sure he is.

But just in case, I let Grant ring the doorbell before I swing the door open.

Grant stands on the porch, looking as good as always. I wave him inside.

Harrison watches us, still leaning against the wall, and when he meets Grant's eyes he gives him one of those guy head nods.

With no choice, I introduce them. "Grant, this

is Harrison, my older brother's friend. Harrison, this is Grant, my..." I stumble, not sure what he is. Friend seems like a stretch. Acquaintance sounds lame. I can't call him the hot guy I've been crushing on since freshman year, but—really—what else is he?

I let the introduction slide because the guys are already exchanging greetings. And it's awkward. Very awkward.

Luckily, Mom steps into the foyer, which saves me from dragging Grant into the kitchen.

"You must be Grant." She smiles, obviously relieved he's clean cut and well dressed.

"Yes, Ma'am," Grant says. "It's nice to meet you. You have a lovely home."

Harrison makes a face while Grant's attention is on Mom. I narrow my eyes at him, staring him down in a warning. In response, he only grins and pops the rest of the carrot stick in his mouth.

"Have a good night, Lauren," Harrison calls over his shoulder as he leaves the foyer.

I watch his back, silently seething.

"Are you ready?" Grant asks after he and Mom finish their polite introductions.

"Yes."

I wave goodbye to my mom, retrieve my costumes from my car, and soon we're on our way to the school.

Two hours later, I stand backstage, waiting.

The lights slowly dim over the auditorium, alerting the audience that we're beginning. The low rumble of conversation dies off, and an expectant silence follows.

Just like always, I'm battling a small bout of nerves. It doesn't matter how many times I walk on this stage; I'm always a little scared of opening night.

The lights rise, and I'm on.

The night passes in a blur. I remember my lines, every one of them—even the one I've been struggling with, but I did trip on a random cord that should have been tucked away behind the wing curtains.

I have a feeling it was Grant's mistake, though, so I don't bring it up with the tech crew.

Actors rush forward in groups, bowing for the curtain call. I wait with Tyler toward the back, ready for my moment on stage. It might be a tad bit vain, but it's my favorite part. I love having the lead, being the one with the loudest applause.

Not that I haven't done my share of chorus parts. I have. But I did my time, and now the spotlight's mine.

Riley rushes out with Brad. The two of them get a huge amount of applause for the small parts they had, and I cheer the loudest.

Finally, it's my turn. Tyler and I join hands and step out. With a flourish, he bows low, and I give a large, sweeping curtsy.

The crowd roars, and I bask in their applause.

My father stands at the front of the stage, waiting for me with flowers. I dash forward to accept them, and then I almost stumble off the edge.

Right behind him, Grant waits with a huge bouquet of roses. He flashes me a smile that's been known to make girls weak in the knees, and I'm sure I'm grinning like a fool.

As a group, we do one last large bow, and then the curtains swing shut. Thus begins the mad dash from backstage, through the school halls, and out into the foyer where the crowd is just starting to trickle out.

This would be my second favorite part—the total strangers who come up and tell me what a fabulous job I did.

Holding my flowers like an award, I thank them, hug them (only the little old ladies), and soak up the praise. By the time my parents filter from the auditorium, I'm beaming. My smile freezes because Harrison is right behind them.

What's he doing here? Nobody told me he was coming.

Good thing. If I'd known he was out there, I would have probably tripped on a flat.

Mom rushes up to give me a hug, and I have to avert my head to the side so I won't smear bright red lipstick on her. Dad laughs and wraps his arms around us both.

Harrison hangs back, looking awkward. Over Mom's shoulder, I notice he's holding something in his hand.

Shasta daisies.

My heart stutters suddenly, and I blink at him. His mouth curves in a tight smile, and he gives me a small wave. One of those waves where your arm doesn't move, just your hand.

I watch, half-frozen in place, and wait for him to give me the daisies.

He doesn't know anyone else in the place; surely they're for me.

Finally, he joins us, flowers still in hand.

I try not to look at them, try not to focus on them. Why hasn't he given them to me yet?

Why? Why?

Our eyes meet, and he looks like he might be about to hand me the daisies when Riley bounds up, closely followed by Grant.

I look away from Harrison feeling...guilty, I think.

"You were awesome!" Riley gushes, and then she too pulls me into a hug.

Then, smooth as ever, Grant slides me out of her arms and pulls me close to his very nice chest. "You really were, Lauren."

He smells like soap and boy and dreams come

true. And I could enjoy it if Harrison wasn't standing right there, judging me.

I can feel his eyes boring into the back of my head.

Giving Grant a little pat, I step out of his arms. "Thanks." I look down at the roses that I've been careful not to crush since the assault of embraces. My cheeks get warm. Lowering my voice, I add, "And thank you so much for the roses. They're beautiful."

With a playful shoulder bump, Grant says lightly, "Just like you."

Riley's eyes are the size of dinner plates, and she's wearing that wistful, far-off expression she gets. If she didn't have her hair up in a bun, I know she'd be running her hand down her braid like she always does when she's really into the romantic part of a movie. In the absence, she clutches her hands at her chest.

I blush and look away, completely unsure what to say.

Riley saves me by sighing and turning her attention to Harrison. Immediately, her eyes stray to the daisies.

The daisies that are still in his hands.

The daisies that he's now holding like he has no intention of handing over.

"That's an interesting accessory." Riley's gaze is fixed on Harrison with such longing that I want to roll my eyes.

"Uh...yeah," Harrison answers. His eyes flicker to me for the briefest moment, and then they look back at Riley.

Riley chews her lips. Obviously deciding that if the flowers were for me, he would have already given them up, she says in her playful way, "They're not for me, are they?"

She says it like she's just teasing, but there's so much unveiled hope in her voice, even Dad looks a tad bit uncomfortable.

For the briefest moment, Harrison's eyes meet mine. Then his gaze flicks to Grant, who, at some unknown point, slid his arm around my back.

Harrison looks unsure for half a moment, but then, as if he can't dash Riley's hope, hands the daisies over. "They sure are."

My heart stops. It just...stops. I blink, suddenly overcome with...joy.

Yes, that's it.

Riley accepts the small bouquet with such enthusiasm, I'm stabbed with a sliver of remorse over feeling so jealous about it.

Jealous?

No. I don't mean jealous.

Vain. Yes, that's better. I wanted the flowers because I was the lead, and they should be mine. And that's horrible. I should certainly work on quelling this unpleasant quality.

"Mr. Alderman, do you think it would be all right if I drove Lauren home?" Grant asks from my side.

My dad smiles, obviously impressed with Grant's manners, and agrees.

Before Grant leads me away, I glance at Harrison. He's not paying me any attention because he's laughing at something Riley's just said.

Another twinge.

"You ready?" Grant asks, and he holds his hand out, waiting for me to take it.

I hesitate for only half a moment before I slide my hand in his.

Grant drives home, and he definitely takes the long way. Also, for a teenage guy, he's sure driving like a slow old woman.

He looks regretful when he finally pulls up to my house.

"Thanks for the ride," I say.

Grant nods and runs a hand through his blond hair. "Maybe I can pick you up again tomorrow?"

"Sure," I say, nodding. When Grant shifts his knees my way, turning his body toward me, I open the latch and slide out of the door. "I'll see you tomorrow."

For the briefest moment, disappointment flashes over his face, but he quickly chases it with an easy smile. "Goodnight, Lauren."

Nodding again, I wave and run up the steps to the front door.

Mom and Dad aren't home yet, so the house is dark. I flip on lights as I make my way up to my room.

As I'm pulling on my soft, fleecy owl pajamas, the front door opens and closes.

"I'll be down in a minute," I call down the stairs.

I'm sure Mom's already in the kitchen, starting the popcorn that she always makes after an opening night. It's a tradition.

There's a knock at my door.

"Come in," I call.

The door opens, and I turn, expecting Dad to be standing there, ready to ask if I want kettle corn or regular. It's not Dad.

It's not Mom either.

My fingers fumble the earring I'm pulling out, and the back falls to the floor.

"Um, hi." I drop to my knees and search for the tiny silver piece.

Harrison steps over and kneels in front of me. He finds the earring back first and holds it up. Our eyes meet, and I can't look away.

Slowly, he takes my hand, turns it palm-side up, and drops the earring back into it. Then he says in a slightly lowered voice, "Nice pajamas."

I jerk up, putting a good amount of distance between us. "They're comfortable."

He raises his eyebrows instead of answering.

"What are you doing up here?" I turn to my jewelry box on the vanity and drop the earrings into the jumbled mess.

"What is all that?" Harrison asks from behind me. "How many earrings do you own?"

What is wrong with him? Doesn't he understand personal space? He's closed the distance between us, and he's leaning over my shoulder. If I were to turn, my lips would just brush his jaw.

I snap the lid closed. "A lot. They kind of took over."

He picks the lid up again and peers inside. "How do find your necklaces when they're all tossed in there together?"

There's the slightest scent of the cologne he wears wafting from him, and in a self-destructive move, I tilt my chin toward him just slightly and subtly breathe him in.

Just as my eyes are half closed in appreciation of how incredibly good he smells, he looks over. Instantly, I force my expression to drop to vague.

"Oh," I say when I realize he's expecting an answer. "I don't like necklaces. It always feels like they're choking me. Scarves are soft, so I wear those instead."

He nods and looks back at the box. "You need something different for this."

I shrug. "Why change something that works?"

Did he just shift closer?

"Perhaps, this used to work for you—" He motions to the jewelry box, and then he turns his head again. Our eyes lock. "But maybe it doesn't suit you anymore. Maybe you need something new."

My stomach clenches.

"Sorry about the daisies, by the way," he says, his tone going back to friendly and neutral. "They were for you, but your friend didn't have any. I didn't want her to feel bad."

I swallow. "Oh...that's okay."

He nods and takes a step away. Suddenly I can breathe again, but now I'm lightheaded.

"You didn't really need them when you had those anyway." Harrison nods to the bouquet of roses sitting on my vanity.

I turn to my mirror and comb my hair so I won't have to look at him.

"Just between you and me," I say. "I liked your daisies just as much." I can't help it, I glance at him in the mirror.

A quick smile crosses Harrison's face, and our eyes meet in the reflection.

"I know," he says. "They're your favorite."

Chapter Six
December 11th

"You would think they could let up on the homework since winter break is only a week away," Riley complains as we navigate down the crowded halls.

I shrug. I already finished the project in my language arts class, so I don't have anything to do this weekend except work on my blog and do the mandatory online career aptitude test that I've been putting off. Mr. Evertson, our school career counselor, reminded me I have to complete it by Monday. Most people manipulate the questions, hoping to get the career choice they want. I have no clue what I'm interested in, so I'll probably end up with something awful like waste management technician.

"I shouldn't have taken Mrs. Majors," Riley continues. "Everyone warned me."

A group of freshman boys stands near us, and

their eyes follow Riley down the hall. She notices and gives them a wave as we pass. They practically swoon at her feet.

It's the cheerleader outfit. They simply can't help themselves on Fridays when all the girls on the cheer squad wear them.

"What are we doing tomorrow?" Riley asks.

"I thought you were doing homework."

She shrugs. "I'll finish it tonight."

I roll my eyes. "If you can get it all done tonight, why were—"

I'm interrupted by Riley's low warning screech. I follow her gaze, and there's Grant. Coming our way.

I shift my backpack and try not to look frazzled. We've been spending more time together since the play, and he's taken to joining us for lunch. But I'm not quite comfortable around him yet.

"Lauren, can I talk to you?" he asks once he reaches us.

From our right, a group of sophomore girls giggle.

Trying to look confident and unruffled, I say, "Sure."

Riley waves her goodbyes and gives me a stern look that I read as, "Call me the minute you get in your car or I will hunt you down."

Grant and I walk through the parking lot, side by

side.

I fidget with my keys. "What's up?"

"You want to go out with me tomorrow?"

He says it with confidence, like he doesn't think I'll say no. Still, his lips are tight like he's bracing himself for a rejection.

The coat I wore today was more for style and less for warmth, and I wrap it closer around myself to block out the December chill. "What do you have in mind?"

Grant leans against my car. "Dinner? Maybe a movie?"

I bite my lip, trying not to smile at how cute and uncertain he looks. "All right."

He grins now, and his face lights up.

"I'll have to ask my parents," I warn. "They're kind of..."

"Protective?" he offers.

I nod, smiling. "The downfall of being the baby."

"That's okay. Call me tonight? Let me know what they say?"

"I will."

He opens my door for me and gallantly motions me inside.

Once in the car, I completely forget to call Riley. It doesn't matter because I find her parked in front of my house, flirting at Harrison, who's hanging Christmas lights with my dad.

She's completely enamored.

"You guys are home early," I say to both Dad and Harrison, but it's Harrison I'm really talking to.

"I went in early," Dad reminds me.

"I had an early afternoon meeting with the university," Harrison says. "So I got off early."

"They were keeping me company while I was waiting for you," Riley says. "I knew you'd forget to call."

"Come on." I tug her arm so she'll follow me inside.

Once we're in my room, she asks, "So, what did Grant want?"

"He asked me to go to dinner and a movie tomorrow."

Riley squeals. "I knew he was going to! He mentioned it to Evan who told me in zoology."

"Then why did you ask?" I begin to organize the bottles of nail polish on my vanity.

Riley flops on my bed. "I want details!"

I shrug. "I don't have any yet. He didn't say where we're going."

She narrows her eyes. "You're excited, aren't you?"

Poppy Red goes next to Pink Blush. My hand hesitates on the bottle, and I begin to wonder if I should alphabetize the nail polishes instead of sorting them by color.

"Lauren?"

"Yes, I'm excited," I automatically say.

Glittery top coats need to be grouped separately from the clear.

Riley flops back on a pillow and pulls Penelope in her arms. The cat meows and then burrows next to her, purring.

"You've loved Grant for, oh, I don't know, *forever.*"

So why do I feel like running away every time he gets close?

Mom pokes her head into my room. "We're going out for dinner tonight. Do you want to join us, Riley?"

Riley hops up. "I'd love to!"

Mom smiles. "Be downstairs in five minutes."

It's our first family dinner out since the play ended. Riley pokes around in my closet as I change out of school clothes.

"So," she says in a nonchalant voice that automatically puts me on edge. "Do you know if Harrison is seeing anyone? Girlfriend back home, maybe?"

I freeze with a comb halfway through my hair. "I don't know."

She nods as if she couldn't care less, but I know better.

"He's too old for you," I can't help but add.

Riley rolls her eyes. "Three years isn't that much."

"Four years," I remind her. "You're not eighteen yet."

"He's twenty-one?"

I tap my fingers on the vanity. "Well, not technically. But he will be in March."

She leans forward as if I've answered my own question. "Well, I'll turn eighteen in April, so that's not so bad." Then she looks at me. "You know when his birthday is?"

Shrugging into a jacket, I don't quite meet her eyes as I walk to the door. "It's only a week from Brandon's. They usually shared a party."

There's a line between Riley's eyes as she studies me, but after she mulls over my answer, the strange look leaves her face.

Mom and Dad discuss restaurant options, and Harrison leans against the couch, adding comments here and there. I hadn't realized he was coming with us.

But I should have known.

We decide on the barbecue place across town, and then we all pile into Mom's SUV. Dad and Mom sit up front, which leaves us three to figure out the seating arrangement in the back.

Riley takes the seat behind Dad, and Harrison is about to slide over to the middle. Right next to her.

"I'll sit in the very back," I offer, already brushing in front of him so I can crawl over the seat.

Harrison sets his hand on my arm and tugs me back. "There's room for the three of us."

Yes, but I don't want you that close to Riley.

"You're too tall to sit in the middle," I argue.

He motions me in with his head. "Then you sit in the middle."

I don't want to be that close to you, either.

Harrison gives me an expectant look, raising his eyebrows as if he's wondering why I'm still standing outside the door in the gently falling snow, blinking at him like a deer.

After a moment, I snap out of it and slide across the seat. Dad thankfully started the car early, so the leather is warm. Riley glances around me, giving Harrison another wistful look, and then she scoots toward the door so I can hook my seatbelt.

Unfortunately, I have to slide closer to Harrison because the buckle has slipped between the seats.

"Sorry," I murmur as my leg pushes flush against his.

As soon as I have it clasped, I inch closer to Riley so he can hook his buckle. He has enough decency to look embarrassed as his fingers accidentally brush my hip.

While she waits for us to finish, Riley drums her

fingers on her thigh. As Dad pulls out of the drive, I shoot her an apologetic look.

She gives me a tight smile, and then she sends Harrison another longing glance over my shoulder. He's too busy tapping away on his phone to notice.

With our coats and scarves, we're packed in the seat like sardines. I'm pushed up against Riley, but there's still no escaping Harrison. Our shoulders are pressed together, and though I've tilted my knees toward Riley, my hip is still resting next to his.

"Brandon's going to be flying home next Friday," Mom says from the front.

Oh, joy.

Actually, I am excited to see my brother, but I'm not sure I'm excited for his reunion with Harrison. They're both obnoxious by themselves; I can't imagine how awful they'll be when they unite forces again.

"He says he wants to go snowboarding while he's here," Dad adds.

Riley squeals—she loves snowboarding.

I scrunch my nose.

"Still hate snow?" Harrison asks.

I give him a sideways look. "I don't hate snow."

Yes, I do.

"You hated it when we were young."

This time, I turn my full attention on him. "No, I hated it when you stuffed snowballs down the back of my coat."

Harrison grins at the memory, his eyes still on his phone. "You had the loudest, shrillest shriek."

"You're one to talk. Remember that time when we were camping, and Brandon sneaked up on your tent—"

Riley very quietly, very demurely, clears her throat. In return I clear my own throat before I finish, saying, "Anyway. I don't hate snow."

At that, Harrison looks up from his phone, and our eyes meet. He wears the tiniest of smiles—as if he just knows I'm lying. Something passes between us, and my mouth goes dry.

His phone chimes with a text, and I reluctantly pull my eyes away.

What is wrong with me?

I have a date with Grant tomorrow night.

Grant, who, as Riley so kindly reminded me, I've been in love with forever.

I fall silent for the rest of the drive, and Riley leans in front of me, batting her eyes at Harrison and cooing over his every word.

It takes forever to reach the restaurant, but when we finally do, I practically crawl over Riley's lap to be out of the middle of them.

My dad notices and laughs. "In a hurry?"

"Just hungry," I answer.

Mom called ahead, and we're seated in less than five minutes. Harrison sits directly across from me, and Riley ends up next to him. Mom slides into the booth next to me, and Dad sits in a chair on the end.

If my parents think it's odd that Riley chose to sit next to Harrison, they don't make any show of it.

"They forgot your crayons, Laura-Lou." Harrison smirks over his menu.

I open my mouth to retort, but, again, I have nothing. Instead, I just glare at him. I wait for the waitress to take our drink orders, and then, still watching Harrison, I announce, "I have a date tomorrow."

My parents look up from their menus, and then my father says, "With whom?"

"Grant." I turn my attention to my dad. "You've met him."

Dad nods. "Kid with the roses."

I bristle at him calling Grant a kid, but I shake it off. "That's right."

Harrison's studying his menu, paying me no attention.

"Where are you planning on going?" Mom asks.

Even though we've been to this restaurant a dozen times, I study my menu. "Dinner. Maybe a movie."

Dad makes a sound in the back of his throat, a sound I don't like.

I look up. "Daddy, come on."

"We don't know anything about him."

"Mom talked with him," I argue. I turn to her. "He's nice, right?"

She nods. "He's very nice."

Dad sighs, closes his menu, and smiles at me. "All right, but I want you to double, just this one time."

I grimace and then look at Riley. "You want to crash my date?"

A slow smile builds on her face, and then she lowers her eyes and plays with the edge of her napkin. "I'd love to...but I'm just not sure who I could ask with such short notice."

Her eyes flick to Harrison, who's still pretending to ignore the conversation.

I hold my breath, wondering how this will play out, not sure how I want it to.

As if he can sense her attention, Harrison glances at Riley. She looks at him shyly—a patented Riley move. I almost roll my eyes.

Immediately, Harrison's gaze slides to mine. He holds it for several moments, his expression cryptic, before he looks back at Riley and gives her a friendly smile. "I don't have plans tomorrow. I could take you if you'd like."

Riley's whole face brightens at the idea—as if it weren't hers in the first place. "Would you?"

He nods.

We discuss it further, and as Harrison is ordering, Riley shoots me a joyful look of triumph. I smile back, but the expression only makes my cheeks hurt.

She doesn't seem to notice my lack of zeal, and she orders her dinner with bright eyes and pink-flushed cheeks.

Harrison's coming on my date with Grant. Won't this be fun?

Dinner comes, but I'm not as hungry as I was a few minutes ago. I nibble on my chicken and push my coleslaw back and forth. I end up wrapping most of it up in a box.

Riley heads home as soon as we get back. Before I go up to my room to call Grant, I toss my box of leftovers on the counter.

On my way up, Grant answers on the second ring.

"My parents said yes on one condition," I say.

"What's that?" His voice is wary.

I sit on my bed and tuck my legs under me. "They want us to double with Riley."

"That's not so bad," he says, obviously relieved.

That's what he thinks.

We decide on a restaurant and then agree on a time for him to pick me up. When we end the call, I sit with the phone in my lap and stare at the abstract pink and gold canvas on the wall.

I should pick out what I'm going to wear tomorrow…and the accessories to go with it…and decide how I'm going to do my hair. It's only eight-thirty. I have plenty of time to do my nails before bed, too.

My eyes wander to a half-finished paperback on my dresser, and I find myself changing into pajamas and crawling into bed, book in hand.

I can do all that tomorrow.

My eyelids grow heavy. The book is about to smack me in the nose when Dad knocks on the door frame and sticks his head in the room. "Your mom made chocolate chip cookies. There are some cooling downstairs if you want one."

The mention of chocolate makes my stomach growl. I toss my book aside and descend the stairs. The brown sugar and vanilla smell hits me as soon as I'm in the hall.

Just as I expected, Harrison's already in the kitchen, helping himself to my mother's cookies. Spatula in hand, she smiles at me when I enter.

"I picked up a new jug of milk this morning," Mom says.

Noticing my forgotten leftovers sitting on the counter, I slide the box in the fridge while I search for the milk.

"I don't know if you should save that." Harrison

narrows his eyes at the box. "It's been sitting there for awhile."

I roll my eyes and grab the milk. "Yeah, okay."

Harrison, uncharacteristically not wanting to argue, only shrugs and helps himself to another cookie.

"Where are we going tomorrow?" he asks.

With half a cookie shoved in my mouth, I stare back at him in question.

"For our date?" he supplies.

And my stomach lurches. The cookie suddenly seems dry and crumbly, and I have to gulp down a swig of milk to help it go down.

He doesn't mean *our date*. He means *the date. T*he date we're going on together but separately. The date that we're mutually going on with other people.

Shut up, Lauren.

Even my brain is against me.

Not quite meeting his eyes, I mutter, "Tuscany's."

"What time should I pick up Riley?"

Why are these cookies so dry?

After I chew about a billion times, I finally swallow. "Five thirty. We'll meet at the restaurant at fifteen till six."

"Early date."

"Busy restaurant," I retort, and then I thank Mom for the cookies and escape upstairs.

A text comes through on my phone. Sighing, I set my book aside and crawl across the covers to retrieve the phone off the floor, where it fell next to the wall charger.

Does Harrison like blue or red better???

I glare at my phone as I type an answer back to Riley. *I don't know.*

Is the red dress with my new heels too much for a first date?

Pursing my lips to the side, I mentally scan her closet, trying to remember which red dress she's talking about. It's the short one, the one with the bordering-on-too-low front.

Yes, I type back.

Two seconds later, my phone rings.

"What should I wear then?" Riley asks.

A visual of Riley in a nun's habit pops in my head.

"Dressy casual," I answer.

Riley somehow growls and laughs at the same time. "You are no help."

I shrug even though she can't see me.

"What are you wearing?" she asks.

"I don't know." I wrap the charger cord around my finger, let it drop, and then do it again. "I'll figure it out tomorrow."

"You're hopeless," she answers.

I grunt a reply. Riley goes on about her outfit

choices for a good twenty minutes before she finally decides. Before she can get started on what she'll do with her hair, I say goodbye.

Exhausted from the conversation, I switch off the lights and crawl into bed.

As I stare at my ceiling, I will myself to be excited about tomorrow.

Chapter Seven
December 12th

Grant is supposed to pick me up in twelve minutes, and I'm starving. It's the kind of nervous hunger that makes me worry I'll eat everything in sight as soon as we get to the restaurant. And while you want to be a date who eats, you don't want to be the girl who devours two baskets of bread sticks before the salad course shows up.

Mom and Dad are at the gym, being healthy, and I'm searching for leftover chocolate chip cookies. I close the pantry, irritated that I can't find them.

I bet Mom gave the rest to Harrison.

Crossing my arms, I stare out the kitchen windows at the guest house. I should march over and demand he give them back. But then I'd walk in on him getting ready for his date with Riley.

My stomach growls at the thought. Frowning, I

turn to the fridge.

And there, sitting on the middle shelf, is my box of leftovers. Grateful, I take it out, dig a fork from the drawer, and help myself to leftover coleslaw. It's not as good as it was last night. The cabbage and carrots are kind of lifeless; the dressing has made everything a touch soggy.

Still, food is food. I take several more bites before I decide that it's just not worth it, and then I dump it in the trash.

Just as I'm looking in the cupboard again, Harrison walks through the French doors.

With my back to him, I demand, "Did you steal the cookies?"

He steps up right behind me—smelling absolutely amazing, I might add—and reaches over my shoulder to the top shelf. "They're up here."

Turning around, I snatch them from him. "Who put them up there?"

Harrison leans a hip against the counter, crossing his arms and watching me open the bag. "Bit nervous?"

I pull several cookies from the bag and then hand it to him. "No."

He watches as I take a large bite and then fidget with my heel.

"Could have fooled me," he says.

"Don't you think you're a little old for Riley?" I

blurt out.

Completely taken off guard, Harrison raises his eyebrows in surprise. "How old is she?"

I slide my feet out of my high heels and peer at them so I don't have to look at him. "Seventeen."

He studies me. I can feel it. "I'm only twenty, Lauren."

I shrug.

Finally, quietly teasing, he says, "If you don't want me to go, I won't."

I bark out a laugh. "What? *No.*" My throat feels scratchy, and I attempt to clear it. "I don't care either way. I just, you know, don't want you leading Riley on..."

"Hmmm." He finishes his cookie.

Why does he have to stand there, looking at me like that? His hair is perfect, as always. His jeans are dark and new, and he's wearing a button-up shirt that he somehow makes look casual and...well, hot...all at the same time.

Still watching me, he crosses his arms and abruptly changes the subject. "Are you wearing that?"

Startled, I look down at my skirt, which is short but far from scandalous. I raise an eyebrow, questioning him.

He shrugs. "You'll freeze. That's all."

But if I wear anything else, I'll look like a dowdy

schoolmarm next to Riley.

I look pointedly at the stove clock. "If you don't leave now, you'll be late picking Riley up."

Feeling self-conscious, I step back into my heels, which are a very tall, tasteful, and glittery pair of gold stilettos. They're rather fabulous, actually.

Harrison's eyes glide from the heels and quickly sweep over my legs. He looks away as if embarrassed and then glances at his watch. "I'll see you at the restaurant."

"Okay."

He stands there for a moment longer, watching me, before he leaves. I exhale slowly as the door closes behind him. Ten minutes later, Grant rings the doorbell.

Somehow Harrison and Riley beat us to the restaurant. Harrison, being all grown up and smart, thought to make reservations, and the host leads us to the back where the couple is already sitting.

And I was right. Riley looks fantastic. She's in skinny jeans and her sky-high black suede boots. Her hair is down and curled, and her eyes are just the right amount of smoky.

Together, she and Harrison look amazing. And cozy. So very cozy.

Harrison stands as we get to the table, and he and Grant do the obligatory reintroduction thing. Super awkward.

As they talk about some sports team, Riley leans forward. "Love the shoes. Did you glitter them?"

"They came this way," I admit.

That's one lovely thing about the Christmas season and its plethora of holiday parties—there's glitter galore.

Grant and I order our drinks, and as we're waiting for them, Riley very casually sets her hand on Harrison's wrist. I zero in on it, and my stomach lurches.

Next to me, Grant gets a text. He frowns at his phone, types something back, and then tucks it away.

"Is everything all right?" I ask.

He gives me a smile, but something tells me it's not completely genuine.

"It's nothing to worry about right now," he answers.

I nod, unsure what to say. Luckily, the waiter brings our drinks. I take a sip of my soda, and my stomach lurches again, this time not from the adoring look in Riley's eyes.

Something in my expression must tip Riley off because she asks, "Lauren? Are you all right?"

My stomach churns again. "I'm fine."

I just need something real. I had too many cookies, too much sugar. Feeling faintly nauseous, I slide my drink away. As I do, it catches on a napkin, and the whole soda goes tipping over, spilling everywhere.

But mostly on me.

The waiter hurries away to retrieve something to clean it up, but in the meantime, we attempt to soak it up with napkins. My stomach knots from extreme embarrassment.

When the waiter returns, he finishes cleaning up the mess. He tosses the rag to a busboy and turns back to us like nothing happened. Sliding a pad from the pocket of his half-apron, he asks, "Are we all ready to order?"

Grant's phone chimes again. He reads the text, and his eyebrows knit. He taps something back and sets the phone aside just as the waiter gets to him.

"Oh," he says, distracted. "I'll have spaghetti with sausage."

Just the thought of it makes me start to sweat. Suddenly the smell of the garlic and onions that permeate the air make me feel gaggy.

"And you?" the waiter asks me with a big smile.

"I'll have...I'll have..." Again my stomach churns.

Suddenly, I'm hit with an urgent wave of nausea. *Oh, no.*

I push Grant, urgently coaxing him to slide out of the booth.

"Excuse me," I beg.

Grant looks at me, stunned, but he moves aside.

As I leap out of the bench, I call back to Riley, "Order for me."

And then I walk to the restrooms as quickly as a person can in heels. I get a few funny looks, but I don't care at this point.

Hurry, hurry.

I burst through the door, and, to my horror, there's a line. Several women and one small girl blink at me.

"I'm going to be sick," I squeak out.

A stall opens, and the group collectively waves me in, everyone stepping back just in case whatever I have is contagious.

About ten minutes later, Riley comes looking for me. When she walks into the restroom, she hesitantly calls out my name.

"I'm in here." It comes out as a half croak, half sob.

"Oh, honey," Riley says as she pushes the door open.

Tears run down my face, not only because I'm so embarrassed, but because I feel so incredibly awful. I'm going to die right here, next to a toilet in one of the nicest restaurants in town.

I gulp back another sob. "Can you tell Grant I'm sorry?"

As only a friend of eight years will do, Riley squats

next to me in the tiny bathroom stall and rubs my shoulder. Very quietly, she says, "He had to leave."

He left. I'm the worst date ever. Another bout of sickness takes me, and Riley stays with me, making awkward sympathy noises.

Since we're not drinkers, this is definitely a new experience for us both.

"It's not you," she insists after a few minutes. "There was some family emergency that came up. He was really sorry. Harrison said he'll drive you home."

I hiccup and then start to cry again. "I've ruined your date."

And despite the fact that I've been battling jealousy the whole evening, I do feel really sorry.

"Shhh," Riley says as she helps me to my feet. "None of that."

We step out of the stall, and a woman about our mother's age watches me from the corner of her eye. She frowns, and Riley reads the expression just as I do.

"She's not pregnant," she assures the woman, who looks taken aback to have been addressed.

I gulp back a sob. How humiliating.

Riley soaks a long section of brown paper towel with cool water, and then she blots my forehead. "I texted my dad. He's going to pick me up so Harrison can take you right home."

"Oh, Riley," I groan.

"It's not a big deal. I don't think he really likes me anyway."

I'm such a cow. Here she is, being so nice, and all I've thought about all day is how awful she is for wanting to go out with Harrison.

"Don't say that," I whisper.

She shrugs. "It's all right. He's really nice anyway."

I'm about to say something noble and profound, but, instead, I have to run back to the empty stall.

Ten awful minutes later, Harrison leads me to his truck.

Riley slides into her dad's car, looking at me with worried eyes. "Call me in the morning."

I nod, which is about all I can do at this point.

I'm trying to walk gracefully down the front steps, but all I want to do is hunch over and lie on the concrete. The cold air helps, but it's not enough.

Harrison wraps his arm around me and guides me down.

"I'm sorry," I say to him, repeating the same apologies as I gave Riley. And then I admit, "I think it was the coleslaw. You were right."

"Probably." He flashes me a sympathetic grin. "But don't worry about it now."

He's warm, and I let myself sink against him. Unfortunately, my stomach rolls again.

"Over there, over there," Harrison says,

immediately hurrying me to a trash can near the entrance.

Once I've finished, tears sting my eyes again.

Worst night of my life. Ever.

"I want to die," I whine.

Harrison rubs my shoulders and leads me back to his truck. We stand outside the door, and he peers at me. "How are you doing?"

Unable to help it, tears spring from my eyes as I cry, "I don't want to throw up in your truck."

I'm not sure what he finds funny, but suddenly he chokes back a laugh and pulls me into a careful hug. "The seats are washable."

But that only makes me sob again.

Then, like a knight from a twisted fairy tale, Harrison picks me up and deposits me in the seat. He carefully shuts the door, and I lean against it, relishing the feel of the cool glass window against my cheek.

Somehow, I make it back to the house without another incident. There can't be anything left in my stomach at this point.

The house is dark, and my parent's car is missing from the front.

"Your dad said they were going out," Harrison explains as he unlocks the door for me.

Feeling like death, I blink in the darkness. All I want is my mom, but it would be really rotten to call them and ruin their night.

Harrison flicks on lights as we go through the house. "Go change," he instructs.

Gladly, I slink up the stairs. Just as I'm pulling on a soft pair of yoga pants, Harrison knocks on my bedroom door.

"Are you decent?" he asks and pushes the door open when I say I am. "I have the couch ready for you."

"The couch?"

He gives me a half smile. "Of course the couch. Everyone knows you sleep on it when you're sick."

My stomach gives a little lurch, but it's not as violent this time. I only feel like I might die—not like it's a sure thing.

As he motions me out, he scoops up my soda-stained sweater.

"What are you doing?" I ask.

He holds up the garment. "Washing this. You don't want it to stain, do you?"

Dumbfounded, I shake my head.

"Go downstairs."

Not sure what else to do, I make my way down. I walk into the living room, where the couch is outfitted with a big, fluffy comforter and several other blankets. There's a can of lemon-lime soda on the coffee table and a packet of saltine crackers.

"How are you feeling?" Harrison asks several

minutes later.

Sitting on the couch, wrapped in a blanket, I groan in response. In the background, I can hear water pouring into the washing machine.

He takes a seat next to me and picks up a remote. "What do you like to watch when you're sick? I personally like science stuff."

He flicks on the television and then looks at me expectantly.

"Game shows," I finally say. I know I should be embarrassed, but I'm too exhausted to worry about it.

"Game shows it is." Harrison finds a channel and then sits back.

After several hours, and only one more frantic trip to the bathroom, I'm starting to feel a little better. I must have dozed off because I wake up to hushed voices.

I peel my bleary eyes open and find my parents standing behind the couch. Harrison explains what happened. Mom strokes my hair and murmurs condolences. Whispering a goodnight, Harrison excuses himself.

I stretch my legs out. Though I have more room with him gone, I already sort of miss him.

Chapter Eight

December 18th

"That's Day Six of our Twelve Days of Christmas Craft Countdown." I smile at my phone/video camera and hold up a wood burning pen. "Tomorrow we'll be decorating keepsake gift—"

"This is possibly the lamest thing I've ever seen," my lovely brother says from the garage door. He leans against the frame, giving me a rotten smile that makes me want to punch him in the arm.

Oddly, it seems to have the opposite effect on most females. Brandon's handsome, I suppose. His hair is brown and dark, and he wears it short. His eyes are blue, and he's quick to smile.

Still, I don't quite see what the allure is. Growing up, his room smelled like a gym bag, and he always made a goopy mess of the toothpaste.

"Happy to see me, little sister?" Brandon asks as

he saunters in and wrinkles his nose at my temporary setup.

"Sure."

He gives me an amused look before he glances back at the pink canvas hanging from the pegboard. "Are you still doing that blog thing?"

Blog thing.

"Yes," I say as I snatch a spool of ribbon from him. "And I was shooting it in the guest house until *your friend* moved in."

I say it like I blame him for the whole thing.

Brandon chuckles. "Where is Harrison?"

"Working late."

"Overachiever." He laughs. "Doesn't he know it's almost Christmas?"

"Yes, well," I say primly. "He has to work so he can find a place and move out."

Brandon watches me for a moment, his mouth twisted up in thought. "You don't still have that crush on him, do you?"

With a growl, I smack my glue gun on the fabric-covered card table. "I did not have a crush on him. What's wrong with the two of you?"

I might have one now. But that's an entirely different matter.

Brandon shrugs, already bored of the conversation. "Did you make your peppermint bark?"

I purse my lips, but I can't quite hold back my smile. Peppermint bark is sort of my Christmas specialty. "Yes."

Brandon gives me a big grin. "I knew you were good for something."

And with that, he jogs into the house.

Rolling my eyes, I prepare to redo the last of my video. Just as I'm setting up, my phone rings.

It's Grant.

I scowl at the screen. I haven't heard from him since he disappeared at dinner. Not that I blame him. But he didn't finish up the last week of school, and I've been a little nervous. It would have been nice to know that he was all right at least.

"Hey, Lauren," he says when I answer. We go through the usual greetings, and then he continues, "I wanted to apologize for the other night."

"I'm sorry too," I say. "I had no idea I was sick—"

"My grandma had a heart attack."

The carefully veiled emotion in his voice pierces me. "Oh, Grant, I'm so sorry..."

"She lives in Florida," he continues. "And Mom heard about it right when we got to the restaurant. There was nothing we could do that night but wait for news, but Mom was so upset...and I didn't—"

"It's completely fine," I interrupt. "Please, don't... it's really fine."

"Are you feeling all right?" he asks after a long pause.

I sit on a crate next to a large toolbox. "It was just food poisoning."

"Good." Another pause. "We just got back from Florida."

"Your grandma," I ask. "Is she...okay?"

I wince, unsure if I should have asked.

"Yeah. She's doing all right."

"That's good."

I want to help, but I just don't know what to say.

"So, Lauren," Grant says, his tone implying he's obviously changing the subject. "I was hoping you might want to...I mean, maybe, if you are free...?"

"Yes?" I bite my lip, waiting.

"Get coffee or something?"

"I need to do some Christmas shopping tomorrow," I answer. "Would you want to go to the mall?"

"Yes." His voice is much more confident. "That would be great."

Chapter Nine
December 19th

Grant beats me to the coffee shop where we agreed to meet. Since he's looking at the menu, not paying any attention to the pre-Christmas hustle and bustle going on around him, I'm able to study him.

He's wearing his letter jacket, and his hair has recently been trimmed. He has a jock vibe about him—not that Grant seems rude and conceited like some of them are prone to be. It's that his movements are athletic, strong, and he's tall, one of the tallest in the coffee shop.

And though it should bother me that a group of girls near my age are eying him and giggling, it just gives me a little ego-boost to step up and slide my arm in his.

Grant looks over, surprised, but then a warm smile spreads across his face. The look sets off a very little flutter in my stomach. An almost flutter.

Or maybe it's just a slight warming. Either way, it feels nice to be with him.

"I never got to buy you dinner." Grant gives my arm a squeeze. "Let me at least buy you coffee."

I peer up at the sign. "I don't like coffee."

He gives me what might be a horrified look, and I choke out a laugh.

"I'm more of a tea or cider person," I say.

"They have tea," he immediately says, like he's nervous I'm going to leave. "And cider."

We reach the front, and I order a chai. Grant orders something with extra caramel, and, as I watch them make it, I wonder if it might be good. Surely you can't even taste the coffee with all that whipped cream in there.

After we get our drinks, we find an empty table in the corner.

"How's basketball going?" I ask, only remembering he's doing it because he needed the extra credit in his theater class to keep playing.

Grant smiles wide. "It's great. I think we have a really strong team this season, and..."

He goes on and on and on...but he might as well be speaking Greek. I have no idea what half of what he's saying means.

I smile anyway.

"Are you coming to the next game? It'll be after Christmas."

I swirl my cup. "To the basketball game?"

I don't even go to games for Riley's sake.

He laughs like he thinks I'm playing coy.

"Sure." I take a sip of tea to hide my grimace. "I'd love to."

Oh, no. What am I doing? I hate sports. I loathe them. What am I supposed to do the whole time?

"Yeah?" Grant positively beams at me. "You can be like my own personal cheerleader."

Ew. I mean...ew.

Not that he says it in a creepy way—he doesn't. He says it in a very nice, sweet way. But still.

Ew.

I force another smile.

We finish our drinks and then venture into the mall. With it being the last Saturday before Christmas, it's packed. Across from us, Santa sits, and a line of eager/terrified kids wait with their bored parents.

After about the third store, I begin to relax almost as much as I do when I'm around Riley. Grant's funny and warm, and though we might not have a lot in common, at least he's nice.

He asks about my blog, and I tell him about it, being careful to go light on the details so he doesn't glaze over.

"You're in one of the advanced art classes, aren't you?" he says. "What kind of art do you prefer?"

We're looking at kitchen towels for my mother, and I browse through them, shrugging. "I sketch a little. But I like crafting more. It's fun to make something practical. Something you can do something with."

He doesn't really seem to understand.

"Have you thought about college yet?" he asks.

I frown. "I'm going to the local university, but I don't know what I want to study."

My aptitude test said I should be a credit counselor, and that's not happening. At this point, my college plans still end in marriage and two springer spaniel puppies. The degree part just looks good, but I don't tell Grant that. I have a feeling it might scare away even the sturdiest of guys.

"What about you?" I ask.

He glances at me from the corner of his eye. His expression makes me wonder if he's nervous I'll tease him. Finally, he says, "I want to be a physical education teacher."

I stop right in the middle of the busy aisle, dumbstruck.

I've heard rumors that there are people who like that horrifying class, but I have never met someone who liked it enough to pursue a career teaching it.

"That's cool," I say lamely, at a real loss for words.

Grant laughs at my expression. "I knew you wouldn't be impressed. You took the mandatory two years, and I haven't seen you since."

I like to exercise. I like to hike and do family bike rides, and I'd definitely take a dance class if we had a decent one in town. But I didn't like gym.

Instead of focusing on that, I change the subject. "You've noticed I haven't taken gym in two years?"

Grant stops and turns to me, his lips tipping in a smile that's sweet but somehow serious. "I've noticed a lot of things about you, Lauren."

My heart does one little flip. It's not much, but it's definitely something.

I smile and look away, feeling a little embarrassed.

We continue through the mall, and I buy something for everyone on my list.

When it's nearly five o'clock, Grant walks me to my car.

"I had fun," he says.

"Me too."

He helps me put the few small bags into the trunk. "Maybe we can do it again after Christmas?"

"That would be nice."

We stand here, staring at each other. For a moment, I wonder if he's going to lean in to kiss me. He hesitates, looking really unsure, and then he pats my shoulder.

"Merry Christmas, Lauren."

"Merry Christmas, Grant."

With one more tight-lipped, "want-to-say-more" smile, he walks off to his own car.

When I reach home, I fully expect to find Harrison and Brandon stealing half of dinner out of the kitchen as my mother cooks. Instead, I just find Mom.

"Where is everyone?" I ask.

"Like locusts, they devoured everything in sight, and then they flew off," she says. "Brandon went to visit a few friends from high school, and Harrison is working on something in the garage."

Curious, I sit at the counter and watch her stir something in a pot. "What's he doing out there?"

"We don't know," Mom answers. "He's being very cryptic about the whole thing."

The sound of a power tool echoes from the garage.

"Is he woodworking?" I ask, aghast.

Mom nods. "Yes, he asked to use your dad's tools since there wasn't room to bring his here."

I desperately want to go see what he's doing, but I don't want him to know that I'm curious.

"How was the mall?" Mom asks.

"Busy."

"Do you like this boy?"

I cringe at the question. "Yeah, I like him."

She narrows her eyes at me. "Really?"

I try to give her a droll look. "Yes, really."

Mom shrugs, obviously not convinced.

I wish people would just stop asking.

"Dinner's at six," she reminds me as I swipe a piece of bell pepper from her cutting board and head upstairs.

There's another whine of the table saw, and I pause. I could take a little look. I'm sure he wouldn't mind.

Then I shake my head. Why do I care what Harrison is doing in the garage?

Pushing the thought out of my mind, I go upstairs to edit and post yesterday's video.

Chapter Ten
December 23rd

I sit cross-legged on the floor next to the Christmas tree, watching a Christmas movie I've seen about a hundred times. Brandon's on the couch, making fun of it and tossing popcorn at my head.

Traditions are fun.

Mom and Dad are doing some last minute shopping. It's the day before Christmas Eve, and I'm sure the mall is a zoo.

Dad and Mom took the whole week off work so they could spend more time with me and Brandon. We've been doing so much family time, I've barely been able to get my daily Christmas countdown video posted.

Luckily, I made a lot of the crafts in advance last summer during the break while I was bored. Tomorrow is my last video of the year, and it's a recipe for my grandma's gingerbread.

Our movie ends just as it's dark enough outside for our Christmas light sensor to flick the outside lights on. I toss the remote to Brandon, who looks pretty comfortable on the couch. I don't think he's going anywhere.

"Do you and Harrison have plans tonight?" I ask.

They've gone out nearly every night after dinner since Brandon's been back. When they're not out, and Harrison's not working, Harrison has barricaded himself in the garage.

Brandon flips through channels, not really seeing anything. "No, he's finishing up the project he's been working on."

Curiosity nags at me again.

Obviously disgusted with the choices on the television, Brandon turns his attention to me. "Why? You want to do something?"

I don't spend very much time with Brandon even though he's not nearly as awful as he used to be. And if I'm truthful with myself, I can admit he's a lot of fun.

I'd often get into trouble when I went with one of his schemes when we were young, but he's grown up a little since he's gone to college, and that doesn't happen anymore. Well, not as much.

"I'm making Grandma's gingerbread," I say. "I need it for tomorrow's post."

"You sure? We could go shopping or something."

Wow, he must be bored.

"We'll hang out sometime before you go back to school, okay?" I promise.

Brandon rolls his eyes. "I'm supposed to be the one promising to make time for you in my busy schedule."

I pat his head, grinning. "Yes, but, Brandon, you're just not as cool as I am."

He swats me away, laughing, and stretches out on the couch. After he finds some sports channel, I lose him completely. Leaving him be, I head to the kitchen.

Gingerbread is easy. You mix together some molasses, a lot of spices, flour, sugar, and a few other odds and ends, and then pop the batter in the oven. The hard part is waiting for it to bake. It takes almost an hour.

That's a long time to wait, especially for something as wonderful as Grandma's gingerbread.

With about twenty minutes left on the timer, Harrison comes wandering in, looking for a glass of water. He pauses in the doorway and glances around.

I look at him expectantly.

"Where's your mom?" he asks.

Bored, I look back at my magazine. "Shopping."

He pauses as he pulls a glass from the cupboard and jabs his thumb toward the oven. "Did *you* bake that?"

"Thank you for your confidence in my culinary skills."

I should scoot him away from the oven when he peeks the door open, but he's so obviously impressed, I can't bring myself to.

"It smells good." He gently closes the door. "Gingerbread?"

Nodding, I flip an unread page.

"When will it be ready?" He makes a face after I tell him. "That long?"

I nod, bored.

Mom's housekeeping magazine is as dull as the ones at the doctor's office, and I toss it aside and cross my arms on the counter.

Harrison leans against the counter, his back to the sink, and gulps down the water. He's wearing worn-out jeans, and there's a yellow pencil behind his ear. He's covered from head to toe in small bits of sawdust, and his perfect hair is dusted with fine, powdery shavings.

And he looks yummy—which is a weird thought for anyone who isn't a termite.

"What are you making?" I finally ask when I can't help myself anymore.

"Christmas gifts."

Tapping my finger on the counter, I ask, "What kind of Christmas gifts?"

He smiles over his glass. "The kind you give people."

I roll my eyes and pretend I don't care.

Harrison sets the glass on the counter and wanders back to his project.

Forty-five minutes later, when the gingerbread has cooled enough I can slice a small section of it, I slip out to the garage with a plate and a glass of milk.

Harrison looks up from the workbench, startled to see me.

I hold up the goodies. "I come bearing gifts."

The air is thick with the scent of fresh-cut wood. It's a heavy, prickly smell that makes my nose itch. I peer at the workbench. I've never attempted any form of woodworking, though I have to admit, now that Harrison is out here, I'm a tiny bit curious about how it works.

After Harrison brushes himself clean, he accepts the gingerbread and plops onto a stool.

"You're making cutting boards," I say as I browse his projects.

Made of strips of slightly different colored wood, they're beautiful. I run my hand over them, marveling.

"I haven't finished sanding them yet," he says.

Harrison sounds self-conscious, and I glance at him. He takes another bite of the rich cake and doesn't quite meet my eyes.

"I didn't know you could do this." I glance at his stack of three. "How do you get the different colors?"

"They're different types of wood. I've got maple, oak, walnut, and cherry in those."

"They're really pretty."

"Thanks."

I offer to take his plate after he's finished, but on my way in, I hesitate by the door. "Can I watch?"

Harrison looks over, surprised. "I'm just sanding."

I shift my weight to my other foot. "I know."

"Okay." He looks baffled. "Company would be nice."

The house smells like spices and molasses, and I breathe the aroma in as I take Harrison's dishes to the sink. I'll deal with them later. I run upstairs, grab a jacket and my phone, and return to the garage.

Harrison's rubbing a piece of sandpaper over the board he was working on when I left.

"I've already run the sander over it," he explains, not looking up. "But I like to finish with the fine grit by hand."

I scoot a stool over to the bench and perch on it, watching.

"This has to be boring." Harrison glances up.

It's anything but boring—it's amazing. I can't believe that Harrison made that. That he could create that with his hands.

I shake my head and continue to watch. The time goes by quickly, even though sanding takes forever. He must have so much more patience than I do. I tend to lean toward projects that are, though maybe not easy, fairly quick.

"Are you warm enough?" he asks after awhile. "Your dad has a space heater I can drag over."

The garage is heated, but it's still not exactly warm. Not wanting him to stop, I shake my head and adjust my scarf more securely around my neck. "I'm fine."

As he works on his project, we talk about his home back in Connecticut. His oldest sister is married, and she had a baby girl last spring. His cousin is engaged, and so is his brother.

Again, I squirm at how grown-up his life sounds.

"But your grandparents still live here, right?"

"Yeah, my mom's parents." He brushes his hand against his face and continues sanding. "I'm going to their house for Christmas."

He's left a fine streak of wood powder on his cheek. I stare at it for several moments before I stretch over and brush it away. Harrison freezes under my fingers, his eyes still intent on the cutting board.

I pull my hand back, feeling silly. "You had, uh, a smudge."

Clearing my throat, I turn my eyes back to the

wood. Silence blankets us, and the air suddenly seems thick and awkward.

I shouldn't have done that.

"So," I say, trying to get us back on track. "These are what you've been working on all week?"

"Mostly."

The response is vague, and I want to kick myself for ruining whatever friendly thing we had going.

"So you won't be here for Christmas?" I ask.

He glances at me. "I think I've crashed enough of your family stuff."

"We don't mind," I say.

Harrison looks up, and our eyes meet. "They don't, but do you?"

My throat closes. I should say something witty, something flippant. Instead, I quietly answer, "I don't mind."

His eyes soften, and he leans forward just a tiny bit. "Lauren—"

The garage door opens, and Brandon steps in.

I must have been leaning in toward Harrison because I find myself jumping back.

Brandon's eyes widen, and a strange look graces his face, a cross between shock and smug rightness.

When I dare to glance at Harrison, he looks bored, just sanding away, like maybe he didn't realize we were sharing a moment.

How couldn't he realize it?

"Is she pestering you?" Brandon asks Harrison, acting like I'm a tiresome five-year-old.

Harrison snorts at the irritated look on my face. "Nah."

Just as I'm about to snarl at Brandon, my phone rings. Ignoring the boys, I answer Riley's call.

"Lauren!" she squeals.

I hold the phone away from my head to protect my ringing eardrums.

"Down a level?" I ask as I gingerly return the phone to my ear.

"You're not going to guess!"

"Guess what?"

"Harper surprised us! She's home for Christmas."

I glance at my brother, and my mouth stretches in a Cheshire grin. "You don't say. *Harper is here?*"

Brandon instantly jerks his head toward me, though he's trying to act nonchalant. Harper is Riley's older sister, and Brandon has had a crush on her forever.

"She wants to go skiing the day after Christmas," Riley says. "We have to go! Please tell me you don't have plans."

Feeling ornery, I watch Brandon's face as I parrot, "Harper wants to go skiing the day after Christmas?"

Riley growls, laughing. "Why do you keep

repeating everything I say?"

"Because Brandon is standing right here, hanging on my every word."

He gives me "the look," the look that says, "Shut up little sister or I'll clobber you."

I grin at him and dance a little farther away. Cutting boards forgotten, Harrison watches the exchange with amusement.

In the background, I hear Riley say, "Brandon's still in love with you, and he wants to come." She returns to our conversation. "Oh, and then Harrison will come too!"

The visual of Harrison and Riley all cuddled up in the ski lodge comes to my mind, but I shake it off.

"Harper says it's fine if they come. Oh, and you need to invite Grant!"

And just like that, we're all paired off. Me with Grant. Brandon with Harper. And Harrison with Riley.

"I'll call him, but it's awfully short notice..."

I can feel Riley's eyes roll. "Will you please stop making excuses to avoid that boy? He likes you. He's gorgeous. *Go with it.*"

"Yes, yes. I got it. Goodbye, Riley."

"Oh, Harper says to tell Brandon that she's really excited to see him again."

We hang up, and I pass the message along. The tips of Brandon's ears turn pink, and he hightails it inside before I can tease him more.

The garage is oddly quiet after all the excitement, and Harrison goes back to his sanding.

"You'll come, right?" I ask him.

"Snowboarding?"

I nod.

He waits for several moments before he answers. "Sure."

Part of me was hoping he'd say no. Not because I don't want him to come, but because I don't want to share him.

I shake my head, realizing I'm being ridiculous. Harrison isn't mine.

He brushes the cutting board, examining it as he runs his hand over the edges. "Finished with this one."

"Can I film you?" I ask when the thought pops into my head. "For my blog?"

Harrison's head jerks up, and he says, aghast, "What? Why?"

"Because—look at it." I motion to the cutting board. "It's awesome."

He gives me a wary look. "I don't think anyone is going to be interested in my cutting boards."

"Yes, they will," I argue. "You said you still have to apply mineral oil to them. While you do that, you can explain how you made them."

Harrison looks really uncomfortable. "I don't

want to be in a video."

"What if I only show the board as you're working on it? No one will see anything but your hands."

His mouth twists as he thinks it over. "All right, I guess."

It only takes a few minutes to prepare the video, and then I'm filming. Harrison explains the process, the care he takes in selecting his materials.

The wood readily soaks up the oil. I watch him work, enthralled, captivated by his voice.

Something warms in me, something I can't explain.

When he finishes, I end the video, knowing I'll probably watch it more times than necessary for editing.

"Was that all right?" he asks, his eyes deliberately away from mine.

"It was perfect."

He swallows, still a little unsettled.

I set my hand on his arm. "Thank you."

His eyes are warm when they finally meet mine. "You're welcome."

A smile twitches at my mouth because I already know how he's going to respond to the next thing I say. "Next time we can collaborate on a project. You can make something, and then I'll douse it in glitter."

He looks properly horrified, and I bite back a grin.

Realizing I'm teasing, he leans forward. "That would be an abomination."

"You won't even consider it?" I prod.

He flicks a strand of hair away from my face, and my heart nearly seizes. "I would have to like someone an awful lot to ever let glitter near something I've made."

I laugh, feeling warm from the banter, and decide it's time I leave before I ruin it.

Just as I'm at the door Harrison says, "Hey, Lauren?"

I turn back.

He rubs the back of his neck. "Thanks for keeping me company."

Butterflies take flight in my stomach. "Anytime."

Chapter Eleven
December 25th

On Christmas, you should wake to gently falling snow outside your window and the smell of baked goods wafting from downstairs. Not to your brother sitting on your stomach.

"Brandon, you idiot, get off of me," I screech.

He laughs and jumps up. "Come on. Presents are waiting."

I sit up, glaring at him. "How old are you?"

"Old enough to know that soon I'll be buying all the gifts instead of receiving them."

With a sigh, I pull myself out of bed. Because it's a special occasion, I wrap my pretty robe over my pajamas, the long satin one with the fluffy trim, and tie the belt at my waist.

"You are not seriously going to put on makeup," Brandon says when I pause in front of my vanity.

I toy with a makeup brush. Harrison might be down there.

Brandon ends up grabbing my arm and dragging me from my room.

My parents and Harrison are in the kitchen, chatting over coffee like adults.

Harrison looks over when he sees us, and his eyes light with humor. "Nice robe."

I brush an imaginary piece of lint from the pale pink satin. It might be a tad much. But if it's too much for Christmas morning, then when will I ever wear it?

I meet his eyes and return his smile with a wry one of my own. "Thank you."

He laughs at me silently and then turns to my mother. "I wanted to give this to you before I left."

She takes her time opening the cutting board, and then she gets all gooey. "Harrison! Did you make this?"

He shoves his hands in his pockets and nods. Though he's obviously a little embarrassed by the attention, he looks pleased.

"I love it!" She pulls him into a hug, as my mother is so often inclined to do.

After she fawns over him for several minutes, Harrison checks his watch. "I guess I better go."

We all send him off with appropriate seasonal greetings. As he walks out the door, he flicks the fluffy white trim on the collar of my robe. "Merry Christmas,

Lauren."

"You too."

He watches me for a moment too long, a faint smile on his lips. I can sense everyone's eyes on us. So far, I don't think anything looks out of the ordinary, but if I just keep staring at him, admiring his sea-blue eyes and the pronounced bow shape of his top lip, someone is bound to notice.

I look away.

"All right, guys," Dad says after Harrison walks out the door. "Who wants to do gifts?"

Brandon bounds to the living room like a little kid, and I follow with slightly more decorum.

We hand things out, and the wrapping paper goes flying. Brandon's over the moon about his new phone. Mom loves her whipped cream dispenser, and Dad's happy with his tablet. I even get a little giddy when I open up my gift card—one hundred dollars to my favorite craft store.

There are other things as well—shower sets and games and slippers and more.

"What's back there, toward the base of the tree," Mom asks once we've opened just about everything else.

Dad crawls under and pulls out the package. The box is about the size of a toaster, and it's wrapped in shiny red paper. It even has a real fabric bow.

"To Lauren, From Harrison," Dad reads. And then, as he hands it over, he says, "He must have forgotten to give it to you this morning.

My heart gives a little thump. Harrison gave me something?

"Should I open it?" I ask, feeling all weird and warm and tingly. "Maybe he meant it for a different Lauren?"

Brandon snorts, and I shoot him a dirty look.

"I'm sure it's for you," Mom says. "Open it."

For some reason, I feel very nervous opening this present in front of my whole family.

It's probably a gag gift, though, now that I think about it. Not a big deal. Nothing at all.

I slide the bow off and carefully tear the paper. Whatever it is, it's inside a plain brown box. Carefully, I pull the tape off the flaps and open them. And then my breath catches.

I pull out a jewelry box.

"Oh!" Mom exclaims when she sees it.

Gently, I place the cardboard box aside and set the wooden one on my lap. It's heavy, and there are twelve tiny drawers. I bite my lip as I slide them open. They're all separated into six compartments, perfect for one or two pairs of earrings each, and Harrison's lined them with black velvet.

There's the slightest odor of varnish clinging to

it, and the wood is glossy and smooth.

"Do you think he made it?" Mom asks absentmindedly, her heart obviously not about to burst like mine is.

Not able to find words, I nod. I lift the top lid, and there, just under the mirror, is a tiny carved heart. Filled with glitter.

My breath whooshes out of me.

There's a hastily scratched note and an arrow that points straight to the heart. *"So it feels at home on your vanity. I didn't want your other things to tease it for its lack of sparkle."*

I laugh, biting back a foolish grin.

This is the sweetest, most personal gift anyone has ever given me.

Brandon's looking at me like I've sprouted another head, and I leap up, clutching the box to my chest.

"I'm going to take it upstairs so it doesn't get broken."

Dad nods, not paying much attention because he's browsing his new tablet, and Mom's busy picking up wrapping paper. Only Brandon stares at me, his eyes knowing. I give him a look, a look that begs him for once in his life to keep his mouth shut.

He only grins and turns back to his phone.

I run upstairs and set the box on my vanity.

Then, since there's nothing pressing I'm needed for downstairs, I begin to sort through my tangled mess of jewelry and carefully move all of my earrings. I'm pleased with how nice they look in their own compartments, and I even find a few pairs that I thought I had lost.

And there's so much room left.

Obviously, I need more.

Since there's no one around, I trace my finger over the heart. Harrison's put some kind of clear coat over it, so the surface is as smooth as the wood.

Footsteps echo on the stairs, and I gently set the lid in place.

"Are you going to help make dinner?" Mom calls from halfway up the stairs.

"On my way," I say.

After one last look at my gift, I head downstairs.

It's a family tradition to watch movies in pajamas in the evening. Grandma and Grandpa came over for Christmas dinner, and, as always, they had our new sets for us.

Mine is soft and fleecy and covered in cows. Brandon's got smiling pigs, and Mom and Dad having matching sheep. Apparently Grandma did her shopping at the local tractor and ranch supply this year.

My grandparents have left, but we're on the couches, eating leftover Christmas cookies, when Harrison walks through the door. He comes in the living room, and, without saying a word, gives us all a funny look.

"Go get pajamas on," Dad orders. "And then get back in here."

Harrison laughs, pushes my stretched-out legs aside, and takes a seat next to me on the loveseat. "I'll stay for the movie, but I'll pass on the pajamas."

"Worried yours aren't as awesome as ours?" I whisper as everyone goes back to picking what we'll watch next.

He leans close, his eyes twinkling. "We can't all have cool cow pajamas."

My cheeks flush, and he chuckles as I look at the throw pillow I'm clutching. Brandon turns off the lamp after they've picked out the next movie—a horrible action thing that is bound to be boring. The only light comes from the dull flickering glow of the television and the twinkle of the Christmas tree in the corner.

In the dim room, I'm very aware of Harrison. I shift. Should I scoot over? Give him more room? The way my legs are up, I'm still taking up most of the couch.

I start to move, but he puts a hand on my ankle.

"You're okay."

I freeze, my heart in my throat.

During the opening previews, Mom, Dad, and Brandon start arguing over the last movie the main actor played in, and I turn toward Harrison, glad for the dark.

"Thank you for the jewelry box," I whisper.

He smiles, but he keeps his eyes on the screen. "You're welcome. You like it?"

I snuggle into my blankets. "Very much."

After that, we watch the movie in near silence. I'm so wrapped up in every tiny move that Harrison makes, I'm not even sure what it's about.

Brandon jumps up to turn the lights back on so we can pick out one last movie before we all go to bed. Harrison leans to the side opposite me as the lamp flicks on and rests his elbow on the armrest.

"Lauren," Mom says. "Can you make popcorn?"

She's sitting on the couch, texting back and forth with my aunt.

"Sure," I say, reluctant to lose my seat.

Harrison stands with me. "I'll help."

I nod and walk to the arch that separates the living room from the kitchen. "What else do you guys want?"

Harrison pauses with me.

Brandon gets an awful, evil look on his face, and then he motions above us with a jerk of his chin. "You two are standing under the mistletoe."

Instantly my knees go so weak I have to put my hand on the wall to steady myself. Laughing so they can't tell how bothered I am, I say, "*Please.*"

Harrison doesn't say anything. He only shakes his head, smiles, and walks off to the kitchen like he's much too mature for something so juvenile.

He doesn't have to seem so offended by the idea. After all, it's not a terrible one...

We make popcorn in near silence, and then we gather bowls and sodas in our arms.

"You have all that?" Harrison asks.

I'm about ready to drop everything. "I'm good."

Somehow I manage to make it back to the living room without making a mess. I disperse the snacks, and then I return to my seat. My dad moved out of his recliner, and he's now sitting by Mom. I fully expect Harrison to take the recently vacated chair, but he joins me again on the loveseat.

The lights dim, and I pretend to watch another movie.

Once it's over, it's well past midnight, and everyone's yawning.

"I'll clean this up," Harrison says to my mom as she starts grabbing bowls. "You guys go on up."

Grateful, my parents accept Harrison's offer. Brandon disappears too, but I stay to help.

"Did you have a nice time with your grandparents?" I ask as we move about the living room.

"I did. It was a little weird not spending it with the rest of my family, though."

We drop things in the sink to tend to tomorrow. I tag behind him as he walks back into the living room, but after a quick inspection, it looks like we already got everything.

"What about you?" he asks. "Did you have a good day?"

It was a better evening.

"It was nice."

He nods, and then, slowly, his gaze moves up. We're standing in the archway again, under the mistletoe, completely alone.

My breath catches in my throat, and I don't dare move.

"It probably wouldn't be wise to shirk tradition twice in one night," he says, his eyes dropping back to mine.

I barely shake my head, the only acknowledgment I'm able to make.

With a small, tentative smile, he gently places his hands on my cheeks and leans down. Soft as a whisper, his lips brush against mine.

My world short circuits.

And then it's over. He pulls back a fraction of an

inch, his fingers still brushing over my cheeks. His eyes search mine, a careful, questioning look in his gaze.

I blink at him, my heart in my throat.

"That was a pathetic mistletoe kiss, wasn't it?" he whispers.

I peep an acknowledgment.

"I think I can do better."

Before I realize what's happening, his lips are on mine, and he's kissing me like he means it. I gasp, startled, and then I kiss him back.

His hands are in my hair, on my back. My fingers run up his chest, clutching his shirt.

He growls something low in his throat, which makes me shiver, and I move in for more.

And then one of us comes to our senses. I don't know if it was him; I don't know if it was me. But we rip apart with the same intensity that we came together.

Lips tingling, I stare at him, my mouth slightly ajar. He looks just as disheveled, and he runs a hand through his carefully messy hair.

"Well," he says, his voice low and rough. "Merry Christmas, Lauren."

I mean to say, "you too," but it comes out all mushed together because my voice is still breathy.

He gives the bottom of his shirt a quick tug to straighten it, and then, without another word, he strides through the kitchen and out the back door.

Chapter Twelve
December 26th

"Do you like snowboarding, Lauren?" Grant asks.

"I ski, actually."

Grant smiles and glances over before he returns his eyes to the winding mountain road. "You look like a skier."

What is that supposed to mean?

"Winter's my favorite season," he continues. "I love fresh powder."

I love the comfy chairs in the lodge. I even brought a book.

"Does your family go much?" he asks.

The winter landscape passes by, and I keep my eyes on the snow-laden trees. "Brandon likes to snowboard. But it's not really my parents' thing."

Grant gives me a sideways look. Then he says, in an uncharacteristically perceptive way, "Or yours, I'm guessing."

I shrug. "Riley and Harper love to ski, so I go with them when they ask."

"You and Riley seem close."

"We've known each other for a long time, and we tell each other just about everything."

Just about.

I haven't told her that I had the most amazing kiss of my life last night with the guy she's crushing on.

But other than that.

To be fair, when she asked if she could have Harrison, I said no. By girl code, she shouldn't have kept pressing.

Though, I also adamantly denied having feelings for him.

But how was I supposed to know at that point?

The whole thing is a mess.

It's settled. I'll just have to keep my lips away from Harrison's.

Not that it will be an issue. When we met in the kitchen this morning, Harrison didn't even look at me. We've barely made eye contact at all.

Now him, Brandon, Riley, and Harper are all piled in his truck, and I'm in here with Grant.

Last time I glanced back, Riley was sitting shotgun and leaning over to adjust the radio.

We arrive at the ski resort just before they open,

and it's still incredibly cold. I double wrap my knitted scarf, adjust my thermal headband, and step out of Grant's car.

Harrison pulls up next to us, and the rest of our group piles out. They're all laughing and happy, and Grant immediately joins them.

Harrison stands to the side, his hands in his pockets. He glances at me the same time I glance at him.

For a moment, we share a look that concedes this is weird. Then he looks off, over the mountain. "It's cold."

"Yes, very."

Hands still in his pockets, he rocks back on his heels. "It looks like it might snow later."

I nod. "It does."

"Are you two coming?" Riley calls.

Apparently the group has already moved on toward the lodge. We snap to attention and follow them.

Brandon's already cozy with Harper, and the two of them walk shoulder to shoulder. Grant laughs at something Riley says, and for a moment, I wish the two of them were together.

We buy our lift tickets, and then we go about the arduous task of bundling up—which is just another reason why I don't like snow.

As we make our way to the lift, I notice the air isn't quite as cold as it was when we first got here. Brandon and Harper go first, followed by Harrison and Riley. Grant and I take the next one, and we're on our way up.

The lift is the one good thing about skiing. It's amazing to watch the crystalline world pass slowly below you. I would be happier if I could bring a camera instead of skis.

We make our way down the slope, and then we go up. Then we do it again. And again. We repeat the same thing for a good two hours.

By the time we stop for lunch, I'm frozen and bored.

"The snow is awesome today, isn't it?" Grant says as he bites into his cheeseburger.

Riley enthusiastically agrees, and then Brandon jumps into a conversation about skiing trips of winters past. I nibble my club sandwich as I idly listen.

I wonder if it's too soon to escape to the couches by the fireplace? My book is calling my name.

We finish with lunch, but as the others get ready to go back out, I excuse myself.

"Ah, come on, Lauren," Riley says, bummed. "Already?"

Feeling guilty, I glance out the picture windows. It's started to snow.

"I'm cold, Riley," I say, trying to keep the whine

out of my voice.

She sighs. "All right, we'll catch up with you later."

Feeling like a student who was just dismissed from the rest of her classes, I give Riley a hug and make a hasty retreat before she changes her mind.

The couches are nearly empty. It's only one in the afternoon. Most people are still enjoying the slopes. I curl up in an overstuffed chair, open my book, and plan to immerse myself in it until it's time to go home.

Too soon, Harrison comes to collect me.

"Surely they aren't ready to leave yet," I say as I set the book aside.

With a slight limp, he plops into the chair next to me.

"What did you do?" I ask.

Harrison rolls his eyes. "I fell and managed to pull a muscle in my leg."

"How clumsy of you," I say, laughing.

He leans his head back and smiles wryly. "Thanks for your concern."

I pull my legs under me, getting more comfortable. "Sorry. Let me try again. I'm very concerned that you're so clumsy."

Harrison shakes his head and makes a sound like a low, single laugh in his throat. "Better."

Then I feel bad for him. "Do you need something for the pain?"

"Riley already gave me a painkiller."

Of course she did.

It seems rude to go back to my book, so I begin to browse the Internet on my phone.

"What is that?" Harrison asks, leaning over to get a better look at my screen.

Angling it toward him, I say, "One of my favorite craft blogs. I'm looking for inspiration."

We end up sitting here, side by side, him in his chair and me in mine, browsing craft and woodworking blogs for hours. There are projects that I love that he hates—usually shiny, pink, sparkly, glittery things. And there are projects he likes that I think are a tad boring.

"Your cutting boards are so much nicer than those," I say as I scroll down a page.

Harrison murmurs, not really acknowledging my statement but not denying it, either.

"I think it's the wood," I continue. "They're using all one type, right? That's why it's all one color?"

"You were paying attention."

I was hanging on his every word, but he doesn't need to know that.

Halfway through the afternoon, I leave Harrison and hunt down hot chocolate. As we drink it, I persuade Harrison to tell me more about where he learned his craft.

"My uncle's a woodworker." He gently blows on

the steaming liquid. "When we moved to Connecticut, I didn't know anyone, so I would go over to his house after school."

I think of Harrison at thirteen, the age he was when his family moved, by himself, trying to get used to a new home.

"Is it nice to be back in Montana?" I ask. "Or do you miss Connecticut?"

Harrison rests his arm on the overstuffed side of his chair and sets his chin on it. "In a way, they both feel like home. Your house, in particular, feels that way. It's in our old neighborhood, and I was there so much."

"Are you glad to be back? I mean, would you have ever moved here if it weren't for the position you were offered?"

I'm really asking if there's a chance he'll ever leave, but I don't want to say it outright.

As if reading my mind, he says, "I like it here. I don't know if I would have moved back, but now that I'm here, I don't plan on going anywhere."

Mimicking him, I rest my chin on my arm. The fire grows brighter as the clouds roll in and the daylight begins to fade. Already, people are starting to pack up for the day.

We're just finishing our second cup of hot chocolate when Riley and the group find us.

Riley's practically bouncing up and down.

"Lauren, you're never going to guess!"

Used to Riley's exuberance, I simply raise an eyebrow and wait.

"Grant's grandparents have a cabin near here, and they said we can stay the night!"

Everyone looks excited, but I can't dredge up any enthusiasm.

"I'll have to ask my parents..."

Riley's face falls. "They'll let you, right?"

I glance at Brandon, who only shrugs. "I'm with you, so they might."

Because my older brother is so mature and responsible.

Mom answers on the second ring. I explain to her what Grant's family offered, and then I wait.

"I don't know, Lauren," Mom says, hesitant. There's a pause. "Do you want to? You don't really like snow that much."

Knowing they can't hear Mom's side of the conversation, it's easier to answer truthfully. "Not really."

Harrison, still in the chair next to me, shifts. He turns to our group. "My ankle's killing me. I don't think I'm up for it tonight."

"Do you have a way home?" Mom asks. "Do we need to pick you up?"

I turn to Harrison. "You're headed home? Can I

ride with you?"

Riley looks crestfallen, but Grant looks downright torn.

"If you need a ride home," he says, "I don't mind taking you."

But he really wants to stay. I can tell. And if he leaves, the others all have to come home too.

"I don't mind taking Lauren," Harrison assures him. He motions to his leg. "She might need to drive."

Once it's all settled, I end the phone call.

Grant pulls me to the side. "We don't have to go. If you can't come, I'm not sure I want to anyway."

He does, but it's sweet for him to say.

"Go, have fun. I'll be fine, and we can catch up later."

He glances at Harrison. "You guys never...I mean, you two—"

"Harrison?" My cheeks begin to warm, but I hope he doesn't notice. "We've never dated or anything."

But we have kissed. Last night. And it was amazing.

Grant smiles. "I like you, Lauren."

Feeling squirmy, I say, "I like you, too."

Studying me, he purses his lips as if he doesn't quite believe me.

Which isn't fair, because I do like him. I'm just not sure I like him as much as he wants me to.

"Drive safe."

He pulls me into a hug, which isn't nearly as pleasant as it could be because we're separated by his cold, wet coat.

After Grant releases me, Riley jumps in.

"I don't think he likes me," she pouts.

"Who?"

Riley sets her hands on her hips. "Who do you think?"

I give her what I hope looks like a sympathetic smile.

She sighs. "Sorry you have to go home."

"It's all right."

"You're kind of miserable anyway, right?" She wraps her long, pale braid around her hand.

"I just get cold quickly. Have fun, okay?"

The rest of our group finally breaks away to collect their things.

"Can you walk?" I ask Harrison.

He takes a step and winces. "Yes."

I roll my eyes and duck under his arm so I can help. He wraps his arm around my shoulders, and together we limp for his truck.

"Lucky it's not a manual," I say as he digs for his keys. "Or we'd be stuck up here."

He laughs as he climbs/hops into the passenger side. I start the engine, and then I fiddle with mirrors and the seat.

"You've driven a truck though...right?" Harrison sounds just a touch nervous.

"Yes." I laugh. "I can drive a truck."

Once we're on our way down the mountain and the heater is blowing hot air instead of cold, I dare a glance at him.

"Thanks for taking me home."

He stretches out his leg. "You appear to be taking me home."

"You know what I mean."

He's quiet for a moment. "You're welcome."

The tiny white flakes morph into large, wet clusters. Now that the sun has sunk behind the mountains, the road slowly accumulates snow.

I'm familiar with driving in bad weather, but being in an unfamiliar vehicle makes me a little nervous.

Everything is going well until I hit a patch of ice and foolishly step on the brake. The truck begins to slide, and I yelp, trying to get it under control.

Next to me, Harrison jolts upright. "Careful!"

It's too late. With a bump and several jolts, we end up in a drainage ditch on the side of the road.

I groan and smack my head back on the headrest. "What do we do?"

"Trade me places," Harrison says. "I'll see if I can get us out."

I half crawl, half scoot over the console and then

over Harrison's lap. It's embarrassing and awkward, and if I wasn't so freaked out about driving Harrison's truck in a ditch, I might admit that sitting in his lap isn't the worst part of the night.

Harrison puts the truck in four-wheel drive and pushes on the accelerator. The truck shimmies back and forth, and the tires spin, digging us in even deeper.

Harrison growls, talking to the truck, as if that will help. Finally, he gives up and looks back at me, resigned. "We're stuck."

"I'm sorry."

"It's not your fault," he says, though we both know it is.

When Harrison opens the truck door, a cold gust of wind blows through to my side. He slides out, goes to the front of the truck, does something, and then goes to the back. When he finally gets back in the truck, he hits the accelerator again, trying to get us out. After several more rotations of this, he gives up.

"What now?" I ask.

Harrison pulls out his cell phone and frowns. "Do you have service up here?"

I check my phone, but mine is as useless as his. I shake my head.

He rests his head back. "We'll just have to wait for someone to offer to tow us out."

Chapter Thirteen
December 26th - Cont.

"Wait for someone to tow us out?" I ask, my voice on the shrill side.

"This is the only way back to town. Plenty of people are leaving the slopes—someone is bound to help us."

I don't love his plan, but I don't have a better one, so I stay silent.

"How's your leg?" I ask instead.

Harrison gives me a somewhat guilty look. "It's fine."

"'Fine' like 'I'm a big strong man, and I won't admit that it hurts,' or 'fine' like 'fine?'"

He twists in the seat, trying to get comfortable since we're going to be here for awhile. "The second one."

"But you pulled a muscle...?"

"I did." He nods. "But it started feeling better by the first cup of hot chocolate."

I gape at him.

He shrugs. "Your friend Riley, she's very… tenacious."

Riley, tenacious? Of course she is. She's also gorgeous.

"You don't like her?" I stare at my glove-covered hands.

The snow whirls outside the window, a white blur in the headlights.

"I like her just fine," Harrison answers. "But not how she's hoping."

"Oh."

"I've been thinking about what you said." He clears his throat. "And I'm not comfortable dating a girl who's still in high school."

I meet his eyes. "But you were right. You're not that much older."

"It feels like it, though. Right now."

There's a stretch of heavy silence, and I have a feeling we're no longer talking about Riley.

"Maybe after she graduates?" I ask, and then I hold my breath.

"Maybe." He lets out a slow sigh and looks out the windshield. "But I wouldn't want her to wait, wouldn't want her to miss out on normal senior stuff."

"Like what?"

He turns back toward me. "Like prom, for one."

I look back at my hands. I have my dress picked out, my shoes, my nail polish. I've even already signed up for the decorating committee.

Still, he wouldn't be the first college-age guy to take a senior to prom.

Just when I'm about to point that out, headlights shine in the back window. They steadily grow brighter as the driver pulls to the side of the road.

"Looks like we're saved," Harrison says.

"Do I need to get out?" I ask as he opens his door.

"No, stay here where it's warm."

A man about my father's age gets out of his truck and meets Harrison. They talk for a few moments, stare at the truck, and then the man goes to retrieve his tow strap. Together, they set it up, doing whatever it is that guys do in this situation.

Once they're ready, Harrison gets back in the truck to steer. In the end, I wished I'd gotten out. The truck slides and bounces, and I'm nearly tossed out of my seat when we clear the ditch.

Frazzled, but relieved to be back on the road, I fasten my seatbelt. Since he seems to be just fine, Harrison can drive the rest of the way home.

He gets out of the truck and thanks the man. They talk for a few minutes more, their breath frozen mist in the headlights. Finally, Harrison gets back in.

"Guess I'm driving, huh?" he asks when he sees me settled in.

I give him a knowing look. "You already admitted your leg is fine."

"As much as I liked being chauffeured around, it's probably better." He flashes me a smile as he pulls the truck into gear. "Wouldn't want you to drive us into another ditch."

Pretending to ignore him, I cross my hands in my lap and look at the white road ahead of us, which only makes him laugh.

I wait, anxious for the conversation to return to our prior subject, but Harrison doesn't seem to have any desire to bring it up again. Soon we've strayed far from it.

The hour-and-a-half drive passes quickly, and we're pulling into the drive sooner than I would like. The lights are on in the house, and it looks welcoming and cozy under its layer of snow.

I unbuckle my seatbelt, but I don't open my door. "Thanks for driving me home."

Harrison sits there as if, like me, he's reluctant to leave. Then he looks at me, an unreadable expression on his face. "It was my pleasure."

Subtly, I angle my knees toward him.

He does the same.

"How's your leg?" I ask, buying time.

"It's fine."

I play with my scarf. "You probably shouldn't snowboard for awhile."

He shifts a tiny bit closer. "You know my leg isn't why I came home."

Feeling as if my heart has traveled to my throat, I swallow. "Right. It was because Riley is tenacious."

A hint of a smile shadows his face. "No."

"Because you would have felt uncomfortable in Grant's grandparent's cabin?"

Again, he shifts toward me, but, this time, he doesn't try to hide it. "That's a little closer."

My breathing goes shallow, and I try to draw in more air without being obvious about it.

I lean nearer, pulled to him like a magnet, remembering last night's kiss. "Because you overheard me telling Mom I didn't want to go?"

"Yes."

He's close enough I can hear each intake of his breath; I can see the rise and fall of his chest. His eyes drop to my lips, and a sharp thrill races through me.

"I thought you decided high school girls are off limits," I whisper as I lean forward.

"They are." His breath tickles my lips, making me feel heady and reckless.

"Then what are we doing?"

146

"Breaking the rules."

I close my eyes as Harrison's lips brush over mine. His kiss is soft, carefully restrained. A text chimes on my phone, but I ignore it. His fingers stray to my shoulders, and then he brushes a hand up my neck.

Sighing, I lean into him. Without breaking our kiss, he shoves the center console up and closes the distance between us.

Another text comes through on my phone, shortly followed by one on his.

Growling, he begins to shift away.

I stop him. "They're just catching up because we're back in service. Ignore them."

Nodding, he deepens the kiss.

Then my phone rings.

Harrison gives me a wry look.

Heaving a sigh, I drag the phone from my purse.

"Who is it?" Harrison asks as he browses his texts.

I stare at the backlit screen, and a squirmy feeling dances in my stomach. "It's Grant."

The only noise comes from my phone's electronic ring.

"You better answer it," Harrison finally says.

Nodding, I accept the call.

"Hey, Lauren," Grant says. "Did you make it home okay? The roads were pretty slick getting to the cabin."

I bite my lip and purposely avoid Harrison's gaze.

"We did, thanks."

There's a lot of noise in the background, music and laughter. Over the din, I hear Harper squeal and my brother yell something as he chases her.

"Sounds like you guys are having fun," I say, hoping he'll reassure me he's having a great time.

"Sure," Grant answers, and then he lowers his voice. "But I wish you were here. I wouldn't have offered if I'd known you'd have to go home."

I close my eyes as guilt washes over me. "You'll have a good time."

"We'll be back in town tomorrow evening. You want to do something? Go to the mall, grab a pizza?"

Harrison's watching me, his brows knitted enigmatically.

"I don't know what my parents have planned yet," I say, hesitant.

I can't tell Grant over the phone that we're just not right for each other, can't tell him that I'm fully enthralled with someone else. But even though we're not dating, it still feels like I'm cheating on him.

After I hang up, neither Harrison or I speak for a few moments.

"What were your texts?" I ask eventually.

"One was Grant checking to see if we got back. The other was from work. There's a last-minute meeting scheduled for tomorrow morning to discuss the development of the new shopping complex, and I have to be there for it."

I nod.

"You should go with him tomorrow," Harrison finally says.

Shocked, I jerk my head up to look at him. "What?"

"You might want to turn your phone down." He gives me a small smile, and then he leans back and sighs. "Lauren—I have a meeting with the senior executive of the architectural firm. You have a mall date." He shakes his head. "We're just not at the same point right now."

I open my mouth to argue, but I don't have anything to say.

"Go. Have fun. That's what you're supposed to do your senior year." He leans forward, an earnest expression on his face. "I missed out on all of that when I graduated early. I don't want you to have any regrets."

He gently places his hands on my cheeks and leans in to press a soft, regretful kiss against my lips. Our eyes lock for several moments, a goodbye of sorts. He gives me a tiny nod, almost more to himself—as if he's making sure it's the right decision—and then he slides out his side.

Just before he shuts the door, he looks back. I

think he's going to say something, maybe change his mind.

Instead, he closes the door.

I don't get out until the door to the guest house shuts. Feeling numb, I carefully lock the truck and make the short walk into the house.

Once I'm inside, I wave a quick hello to my parents, who don't notice anything is amiss, and escape to my room. I sink onto my bed, but I don't cry. There's nothing to cry about. We kissed a couple times, that's all.

I liked him. He liked me back. I made him feel like a pedophile.

What's two stupid years? I'm eighteen; he's twenty. Sure, he'll turn twenty-one in a few months, but then I'll turn nineteen in November.

Maybe he doesn't want to take you to something as juvenile as prom, with its bad music, bad punch, and boys reeking of cheap cologne. Or maybe he doesn't want to introduce a baby girlfriend to his colleagues.

The fact that he even has colleagues makes me uncomfortable. I haven't even decided on what I'll be majoring in yet.

Maybe he's right after all.

With a long sigh, I drag myself up and begin the process of removing layers. I stare at my new jewelry box for a good several seconds before I open a drawer and toss my earrings into a compartment. Then, because apparently I like to wallow, I lift the lid and run my hand over the glittering heart.

With a flick of my wrist, I snap the lid shut and pick up my phone.

I dial the number before I can change my mind.

"Lauren?" Grant sounds surprised to hear from me again.

"We're on for tomorrow."

"Yeah?" There's a smile in his voice. "Great. Can I pick you up at four?"

"That would be fine." I rip my eyes from the jewelry box. "I'm really looking forward to it."

There's a squeal in the background—my friends still enjoying themselves, and Grant chuckles. "Me too."

After we hang up, I walk to the window. Harrison's windows are dark, and his truck is gone. Apparently he's decided to move on too.

Chapter Fourteen
February 5th

January has flown by in an unspectacular jumble of snow and schoolwork. Brandon went back to college, I went back to high school, and Harrison started at the university.

Now that we're in the second half of the year, more people seem to be talking about what they're planning on studying in college. Riley's decided on elementary education, and Tyler's looking into several different medical professions.

And me? I looked up a couple of springer spaniel rescue organizations.

Mom and Dad have told me not to worry about it, that you don't have to know right away. But it's nagging at me. I'd at least like to study something I'm somewhat interested in before I get married and settle into the house of my dreams.

Harrison picks up a piece of bacon and studies the stretched out newspaper in front of him. He takes a bite as he circles a listing.

I scoot my scrambled eggs back and forth on my plate, not hungry.

"There's a place near the university," Harrison says. "But it's all the way across town from work. I'd rather find somewhere in between, somewhere near here."

"There's no rush," Dad says, and Mom nods in agreement. "You're welcome here for as long as you like."

Even though I haven't finished the first piece, Mom slides another slice of French toast on my plate.

"You haven't eaten a thing, Lauren. You need to hurry," she says. "You're going to be late."

I nod and attempt a few bites.

"Is Riley coming over for dinner?" she asks as I stand to scrape off the rest of my plate.

"There's a game tonight," I answer.

She nods, and I can practically see her mentally adjusting her menu accordingly. "What about you, Harrison? Do you have plans?"

There's a slight pause before he says, "I have a date, actually."

The words hang between me and him, and he doesn't look my way. My parents don't notice, and they continue to chatter away.

It's fine. It's been over a month. Not a big deal. I'm practically dating Grant. Why shouldn't he be seeing someone?

"I gotta go." I grab my keys from the counter and escape out the back door.

Once I get to my car, I realize I forgot my backpack. I start the engine so it will warm up, and then I jog back into the house.

When I get back to my car, I find Harrison leaning against it, waiting for me.

I don't quite meet his eyes. "I'm running late."

"Are we okay? I mean..." He shrugs, looking uncomfortable. "Well...are we okay?"

He looks so earnest with his hands shoved in his pockets and his expression guarded. I can't help it; my heart flip-flops. You wouldn't think it would. I was devastated the night he brought me home. But I can't seem to help it.

"Yeah, we're good."

He gives me a nervous smile. "Friends?"

Feeling tired though it's only morning, I sigh. "Sure."

"And you're okay with...?"

His date. Him dating someone. This very mature, very lovely girl he's dating.

"Of course I am." I give him a bright, chastising

smile. "You really need to get over yourself, Harrison." To prove I'm not still hung up on him, I give him a playful swat on the arm. "You're really not so amazing that I'd still be pining for you."

Unfortunately, smacking Harrison's arm just makes me want to step up to him, wrap my arms around him. Maybe lean up on my tiptoes and angle toward—

"Good." He gives me a wry smile. "Glad to hear it."

Hands still in his pockets, he rocks back and forth on his heels. We just kind of stare at each other.

"I really do need to go," I motion to my door, which he's blocking.

"Oh, right." He jumps out of the way and opens it for me. "Have a good day, Lauren."

"You too."

After he closes the door, I give him a nonchalant, "I'm-so-not-in-love-with-you" wave goodbye.

Once I round the corner out of my subdivision, I bang my head against my headrest. Our conversation runs on a continuous loop in my brain.

Thanks to Harrison, I pull into the school parking lot with only minutes to spare. I slam the car door, and when I try to hurry away, my backpack yanks me back. Rapidly running out of time, I growl as I fight with the locks and pull my strap free of the door.

I plop into my seat with only four seconds to

spare. Flustered, I pull out my books, take a deep breath, and then sit back, pretending to be serene.

"Bad morning?" Riley asks from next to me.

Only now do I acknowledge her. She's slouched over, her elbow propped on her desk, her cheek resting on her hand. She smiles, her eyes teasing, loving to see me rattled.

"No," I lie.

"You were almost late." With her free hand, she taps the desk with her pencil's eraser.

Remembering I need a pencil as well, I dig through my backpack. "But I'm not."

She opens her mouth, but she's cut off by Mr. Maxwell, who apparently thinks first period is for American history and not for social interaction.

"Miss Newton," he says. "Would it be all right with you if I start my lesson now?"

Riley turns toward the front. She sits back in her seat and smiles, ignoring the teeters from the other students. "Sure, Mr. Maxwell. Whenever you're ready."

"That's very gracious of you," the teacher says, and then he launches into a lecture on the French and Indian War.

We sit through class, and I try to keep my mind on the battle and off contemplating Harrison's date. I'm failing miserably.

She probably has platinum hair and huge blue

156

eyes. Or maybe her complexion is darker, with olive skin and a long sheet of ebony hair. And she'll be tall, model tall. And I bet she wears heels—simple, sleek ones...no glitter anywhere. She's probably an architect, maybe she even works with Harrison. Maybe she's just a tad older than he is...far more sophisticated than I am...

"Are you going to scowl at your desk all day, or do you think we should get to our next class?" Riley says, standing over me.

I blink at her. "Did the bell ring?"

Riley grins. "Yeah, like, several minutes ago."

Looking around, I realize overachievers from the next class are already starting to filter into the room.

"What has you so rattled?" Riley asks.

I shake my head, not ready to admit why I'm upset. Riley's moved on from Harrison, I think. She's been talking about some guy from one of the other high schools a lot lately. But it still could be a sore spot.

We go through the rest of our morning classes, and, finally, it's noon. Other schools have off-campus lunches, but we're stuck here. Riley and I make our way through the line. Soon after we pick a table, Grant slides in next to me, facing the opposite direction so he can lean his back against the table.

"Hey, you," he says, his mouth tilting in a smirk.

Pushing my earlier agitation aside, I smile back.

"Hey to you too."

"You gonna come to my game tonight?" He tilts his head when I start to decline, and he pins me with raised eyebrows and an expectant look. "No, *no*—you promised you'd make it to one. Come to tonight's."

Basketball...gymnasium...screaming kids and screaming parents...

"Lauren," he draws my name out, half pleading, half reprimanding me for trying to get out of it.

I purse my lips. "I don't know..."

With a smile—and without any notice—he leans forward and presses his lips to mine in a soft, short kiss. "Please?"

I stare at him, dumbfounded and disappointed. That was our first kiss. And it was in the school cafeteria, with Riley and Grant's popular friends watching. With the smell of beef stew and pizza hanging in the air.

But how picky can a girl be? It was a nice kiss. It was.

Not as nice as the Christmas kiss you shared with Harrison...

I shove the thought away and smile brightly. "Yes, of course, I'll come."

Grant's face lights up, making me feel as low as a slug. "Really?"

I nod, trying to look excited.

He turns in the seat, wraps his arm around my

shoulders and snatches unwanted food from my tray. And that's the way we stay until the bell rings.

"Are you and Grant officially dating now?" Riley asks as she fluffs her ponytail.

I watch her in the mirror's reflection as she primps in the school bathroom closest to the gym. "I don't know. I don't think so—he's never said. Maybe?"

She rolls her eyes. "Do the two of you even talk?"

Grant and I carry on pleasant, shallow conversation about the things we have in common. So, no...we don't talk that much. We just walk next to each other in the halls. He's so popular, there's always someone wanting his attention anyway.

"Yes," I say, rolling my eyes.

She turns toward me, flips her ponytail over her shoulder, and poses. "How do I look?"

I run my eyes over her skirt, matching top, and white sneakers. "*Cheer-ful.*"

Riley grins. "That was lame."

Giving her a bored look, I say, "That's the best I can do right now."

She grabs my shoulders and pushes me through the door. "Games are fun! Just look at all these happy people!"

"You can turn it down a little." I give her a wry look

over my shoulder as she steers me through the thin crowd. "Shouldn't you save that pep for the game?"

"I have an everlasting supply." To prove her point, she hops as she continues to herd me into the gymnasium.

If she were anyone but a cheerleader, people would look at her like she was crazy. But she's wearing the skirt, so everyone beams at her enthusiasm.

Trusting I'm following, Riley bounds up the bleachers, finding me what she deems to be the "perfect" spot. I follow, trying to look happy just in case Grant looks my way. He's already here, standing with his team, and they and the other team are doing sporty pre-game things.

"Here you go!" Riley says after she ushers me past parents and siblings and giggling underclassmen. "This is a good spot."

I'm in the second row of the bleachers, right in the middle.

"Thanks." I scrunch my nose at the scarred wooden bench.

Riley rolls her eyes but gives me a real smile that's tinged with a little hurt. "It won't be that bad. I promise."

I nod, trying for her sake to work up some enthusiasm. Riley loves this stuff. I can get through an hour for her sake.

It is only an hour, right? I only have to stand here by myself, looking awkward and feeling out of place, for one hour?

"It would be better if we were, you know, hanging out together," I admit.

"Don't you start that!" Riley sets her hands on her hips. "I tried to get you to try out for cheer—"

"That is so not what I meant." Laughing, I shake my head and wave her off. "Go. Cheer. Be adored."

Out of nowhere, she hugs me. "Thank you for coming to my game, Lauren."

Then she bounds off, leaving me feeling like the worst friend in the world. She's so excited I'm here. Why haven't I done this for her before? She's my best friend. So what if the gym smells like sanitizer and sweat? (And it does. It really, really does.) I should have done this before now.

I stand here, arms crossed, with a big smile plastered on my face, waiting for the game to start. I hope it will be soon.

The band plays the last of their pep song, and the National Anthem begins. At least I know what to do during this part.

Just as we're getting to "rocket's red glare," a family filters into the row in front of me. They all find their spots, and the dad ends up smack dab in my line of sight. There's a group of juniors to my right and a family to my left. There's nowhere for me to go unless I want to get very cozy with someone I don't know.

And I don't.

The song ends, the crowds settle, and just as the game is about to begin, the man puts his huge Stetson back on. All I can see is cowboy hat.

I lean to the side, trying to peer around him. Grant, who apparently lost me in the crowd, spots me. Relief washes over his face. He must have thought I left. I give him a small wave, which he returns with a wink, and the girls to my right all swoon, obviously thinking the gesture was for them.

The game finally starts, and I lean to the side, trying to watch.

The boys run to the right. Then they run to the left. Someone shoots the ball; it misses, and the crowd groans. Off they go to the right again...and so on. The monotony is broken up by the sporadic goal. *Goal?* That doesn't sound right. Maybe it's just called a basket or a point. But are there multiple points per basket? I'm not sure.

It wouldn't be so bad if I could just see. The game pauses as something is disputed. Riley waves at me from her spot in front of the bleachers. She gives me a questioning thumbs up sign, and I return it, feeling about five years old as I do.

I check my phone as the official speaks with the

visiting team's coach. A missed text shows on my screen. I click on it, grateful I have something to do while I wait for the game to resume.

Then I see who it's from, and my stomach flutters—which it really shouldn't do.

Which drawer does your mom keep the ice cream scoop in?

The buzzer goes off, and the game begins again. I hurry with my reply to Harrison. *Drawer underneath the microwave.*

I tuck my phone into my pocket and scan the players for Grant, but he's not playing right now. I frown and try to find him on the bottom row of the bleachers where the rest of the team sits. Another text comes in.

I can't find a saucepan, I read.

Since Grant's not out anyway, I give up on watching the game for the moment.

Why do you need a saucepan for ice cream? I write.

Almost immediately, he writes back, *For hot fudge sauce.*

The image of him and his ultra-smart, supermodel date hanging out in my kitchen, laughing while they make sundaes to take back to the guest house, makes me slightly queasy. I tell him where the pots are, and then I resolve to ignore any other texts.

From my lap, my phone vibrates.

I glance at it and then look away. I hold out for five whole seconds before I pick it back up.

Where are you?

You shouldn't text on a date, I inform him. *It's rude.*

He writes back, *For your information, Miss Manners, my date is over.*

Over? It's not even eight.

Seriously, where are you? Your parents aren't home, and Mom's recipe makes too much for just me.

He doesn't mean anything by it. He's just being nice. With him living in the guest house, we're practically neighbors, so he's being...neighborly.

Basketball game, I write.

Basketball game??? Since when are you a sports enthusiast?

Before I can reply, another text comes in, and, this time, it's a picture of a carton of my favorite Rocky Road ice cream.

I bite the inside of my cheek, refusing to acknowledge the warm feeling that's settled into my chest. Ignoring the picture, I answer his previous question. *Since Grant plays basketball.*

Several minutes go by, and my phone is silent. I'm relieved and maybe a little disappointed. I jump when it vibrates again.

Are you two actually dating now?

I read the text several times, unsure how to

respond, and, frankly, tired of everyone asking. Finally, I decide to go with the truth. *I don't know.*

The crowd jumps up around me, all of them cheering and whistling. The girl beside me screeches so loudly, my ears ring. I cringe away from her.

How can't you know if you're dating someone? Harrison asks.

We haven't talked about it.

He answers, *But you're suffering through a game for him?*

I frown. *I thought you liked sports.*

Immediately, he writes back, *Sure, but you don't.*

What's your point?

Harrison answers, *Before he expects you to act like a girlfriend, he should make it clear that you are one.*

I frown at my phone, growing irritated. Is he jealous? If he is, what right does he have to be? Good grief, he had a date of his own tonight.

I'm just doing the high school thing—which includes going to school games, I write. *Like I'm supposed to be doing.*

Silence. Long amounts of painful silence.

When the phone vibrates, I'm almost scared to look at what he wrote.

That's exactly what you should be doing. Have fun.

His text is followed by a no-hard-feelings, we're-still-friends smiley. I stare at it, trying to dissect his words, his meaning. Irked, I thrust my phone into my purse and refuse to look at it the rest of the night.

The game finally ends after an hour-and-a-half, and I make my way through the crowd to find Riley. Grant and a few of the other players have already joined the cheerleaders, and Grant waves to me as I make my way toward him. He breaks from the group to meet me, and, to my surprise, he pulls me into his arms and kisses me.

I blink at him, startled, and then match his smile with my own. That's the second time today. It's got to mean something. Are we dating, and I just don't know it?

"I'm glad you came," he says.

"Me too."

Riley bounds over. "Did you see the basket that Grant made? It was amazing!"

I missed it. I have no idea what she's talking about.

Smiling, I do the only thing I can think of. I stand on my tip-toes, press another kiss to Grant's lips, and then say, "Good job."

A sweet grin stretches across his face, and he looks so happy, my heart melts a little bit. My conversation with Harrison shoved aside, I happily settle next to Grant as he wraps an arm around my shoulders.

We go out for pizza with the team after the game, and it's after ten by the time I get home. For once, I beat my parents. Mom called earlier and said they were going to a movie and wouldn't be back until late.

Not ready for bed, I wander into the kitchen to make myself a cup of tea. My eyes instantly go to a bowl and spoon. There's a note with them.

You missed some seriously awesome hot fudge, but I might have left some in the fridge for you.

My stomach clenches, and warmth spreads from my chest to my toes. Then I scrunch the note in my hands and toss it in the trash. I'm not supposed to feel this way about Harrison.

I turn on my heel to leave the kitchen, but then I stop. There's no reason to waste perfectly good hot fudge sauce. Feeling like I'm somehow betraying Grant, I make myself a sundae.

And it's good—too good. Too decadent, too rich. Exactly what I want, but exactly what I shouldn't have right now. Dumping it in the sink, I watch the ice cream melt and swirl down the drain.

Chapter Fifteen
February 13th

"After the wax has solidified, you can remelt what remains in the pot and pour it onto the top of the candle to cover any sunken areas." I demonstrate, being careful not to spill the wax on my mother's countertop. "Give it a day or two to cure, and then it's ready to burn."

I finish up the video and then start the task of cleaning up my mess. I run hot water into the pouring pot, and the soy wax begins to melt away. Already, I can tell it's going to clean up much easier than the paraffin that I tried for my first candle tutorial.

I'm carefully packing up my fragrance oils when Harrison wanders in from the back. He sniffs the air and then tilts his head. "What is that?"

"I call it Enchanted Apple."

He spots the candle and then starts to pick it up.

"No!" I lunge for his hand and then laugh at his startled expression. "You don't want to move it too much in the first twelve hours."

His eyebrows rise. "You made this?"

I nod. "Just now."

"There's no glitter involved."

I roll my eyes. "I don't know for sure, but it seems that adding glitter to something you burn might be a really bad idea."

He sits at the counter and crosses his arms on the table. "You could have used spray adhesive on the glass container and given the outside a good dousing."

Slowly I raise my eyes, meeting his.

A teasing smile lifts the side of his mouth. "It was a joke."

"It's a good idea."

"You don't have to add sparkles to everything you touch. You're not a fairy."

I'm intrigued, my mind already working. I choose to ignore the last bit. "You could use stencils…add designs! I'll let this sit until tomorrow, and then I'll embellish it."

Harrison just rolls his eyes, swivels the stool, and goes to raid the fridge.

"I found a place to rent," he says all nonchalant-like.

Like it's no big deal that I'll soon have my space

back. Like it's no big deal that he'll no longer be a few dozen feet away...no longer be here, rummaging in the fridge, bugging me about my glitter addiction.

I swallow, glad his back is toward me. "Yeah?"

"I had to talk the landlord into letting me pay him."

That's odd.

Wrinkling my nose, I lean on the counter. "You had to do what?"

Harrison closes the fridge after he finds the cheesecake Mom made last night. After living here for several months, he's right at home in the kitchen. He retrieves a plate from the cupboard while I get the spoons.

He leans against the counter opposite me, cuts a large slice, and slides it on the plate. "My new landlord wanted to let me stay for free."

I offer him a spoon and then dig in with my own. He doesn't object to me stealing part of his dessert. Not that it would have mattered; I would have done it anyway.

"He sounds a little loony," I say as I go for another bite.

Harrison chuckles. "I'll let your dad know how you feel about him."

I pause, a bite halfway to my mouth. "What?"

He settles against the counter, leaning toward me.

"Is it okay with you?"

"Is what okay?"

"If I stay here, start paying your parents rent. I know the guest house was kind of your area, so I wanted to make sure you are all right with it."

How do I feel about Harrison staying?

"You've already defiled it with your guy junk anyway." I take another bite, this time savoring it slowly, trying to look like I couldn't care less. "You might as well stay now."

When I do look up, his eyes are on me. It's a questioning look, a look that makes my insides do somersaults.

A look that he simply should not be giving me.

His gaze finally drops to the nearly empty plate between us. "Shouldn't you have plans for tomorrow?"

My breath catches. Tomorrow's Valentine's Day.

"Um..."

"You said you were going to glitter that candle." He nods to it. "But shouldn't you be going out with Grant?"

Oh, right.

Grant's taking me out to dinner.

"Of course we have plans."

"Am I allowed to ask if you're official yet?"

Losing my appetite, I set my spoon down and squirm. "We've decided not to discuss it."

"You've chosen not to discuss it?" He gives me an incredulous look. "You mean neither of you have chosen to bring it up."

Yeah. That.

I shrug and slip away from the counter to get a glass of water. He comes up behind me as I fill up the glass, and I focus on the cold water pouring from the filter.

"You don't have to go out with him, you know." He pauses. "If you don't like him."

"I do like him," I say with more force than necessary.

Harrison just stands there, quiet as if he's thinking. He's close enough I could turn around and step into his arms, clasp my hands behind his neck. He'd kiss me back. I know he would.

With my back still toward him, I close my eyes for a moment, imagining it. Then I take a quiet, steadying breath and move to the side, away from Harrison. I can feel his eyes follow me across the kitchen, into the living room.

"I have homework," I call over my shoulder.

And like the little girl he thinks I am, I run away and hide in my room.

Chapter Sixteen
February 14th

"You're sure you don't want to double with us?" I ask Riley, desperate. "It would be fun."

I twist a strand of my hair around my finger, a nervous habit I haven't seemed to break, and stare at my reflection in the mirror. My makeup is perfect, my hair curled nicely. There are no excuses not to go out, but all I want to do is stay home.

"I'm watching the boys," Riley says. "You know I can't get out of that. I volunteered weeks ago so Mom and Dad could go out to dinner."

I rack my brain, trying to think of someone that could watch Riley's younger brothers. Maybe Mom? No that's horrible. I can't ask her to do that on Valentine's Day.

"Besides," Riley continues. "Grant's already made reservations. I can't just show up."

Maybe you could take my place.

I gulp, feeling guilty for the thought. What's wrong with me? Grant's great. He's nice; he's handsome. Every other girl in school would be ecstatic to be in my shoes.

"That's true. You're right." I nod at my reflection, reminding myself to be brave.

It's just dinner anyway.

The doorbell rings, and I jump. It's too early for Grant to be here, so I let Mom answer the door. A voice I don't recognize echoes through the entry.

"I should go," I tell Riley. "I'll see you at school tomorrow."

"Have fun." She says it like a command.

Just as I'm ending the call, Mom yells up the stairs, "Lauren, it's for you."

Curious, I peek my head out of my room. Mom peers up at me from the bottom of the staircase, holding a bouquet of daisies.

She grins. "Are they from Grant?"

I grow hot and then cold. My emotions go from giddy to irritated and settle at somewhere in between. I take the vase from her, and, together, we walk into the kitchen. I set them on the counter and snatch the card before Mom has a chance to look at it.

After I read the note, I stare at it, baffled.

"Well," Mom says. "Who are they from?"

"Grant," I mumble.

"Oh, that was sweet of him."

Mom fusses over the flowers, and I read the card again. *Looking forward to tonight.*

I slide the envelope back in the card holder and then tap my fingers on the counter, staring out the back window. The night is growing dark, and there are no lights on in the guest house. Usually Harrison's home from work by now.

He must have plans for the night.

"When's Grant going to be here?" Mom asks.

"Hmmm?" Distracted, I look over. "Oh, soon."

"I have to get ready." She flips through a stack of mail, sorting it into piles. "Your dad won't tell me where he's taking me tonight."

I know, but I'm not going to ruin the surprise.

"Don't stay out too late," I tease.

She raises an eyebrow, giving me a wry smile. "I'll be back by curfew."

Not long after she leaves the kitchen, the doorbell rings. I bite my lip and shake my shoulders, trying to rid them of the tension that's settled there.

Grant's waiting for me at the door. He surveys my dress with a smile. "You look nice."

Twirling a strand of hair, I say, "Thanks."

"Are you ready?"

I nod, nervous even though we've already been

out on a few dates. This one feels different.

The restaurant is already busy by the time we arrive. Grant takes my hand and leads me through the crowd toward the front. The lights are dim, the atmosphere hushed. A piano plays in the next room.

"We have six o'clock reservations," Grant says to the hostess.

The woman smiles at us. "What name is the reservation under?"

"Grant Walters."

She purses her lips, scans the list, then looks up, concerned. "For six o'clock?"

Next to me, Grant shifts. "That's right."

She shakes her head, looking apologetic. "I'm sorry. I don't have it down."

The line of impatient people push at our backs, and I can practically feel them breathing down my neck.

Grant leans forward, growing nervous. "I made it yesterday. Are you sure it's not there?"

"No, I'm sorry." She looks apologetic. "There's nothing I can do tonight. We're completely booked."

The crowds seem to shift closer.

"It's all right," I whisper to Grant, hoping to ease the panicked look from his face. "We can go somewhere else."

For a moment, I think he's going to argue with

the woman, but then he looks at me, and his shoulders slump in defeat. Slowly, he nods.

We press through the well-dressed crowd, murmuring apologies as we make our way out. We pause once we reach the lamp-lit garden walkway. Right now all the plants are dormant, asleep for the winter, but I'm sure it's lush in the summer. Tonight, it's just depressing.

"I'm so sorry." Grant runs a hand over his neck, looking as tense as I did earlier. "I don't know what happened."

I set my hand on his arm. "It's still early. We'll try somewhere else."

We drive through town, quickly finding out that even the most casual restaurants have an hour wait or more at this point. Grant is growing increasingly agitated.

Finally, an hour-and-a-half later, we end up pulling into a fast food restaurant. If we'd waited at one of the first restaurants we tried, we would have probably been eating by now.

"Do you think we could just go through the drive-thru?" I motion to my dress, which is slightly too formal for a restaurant with plastic seats and a kid's play area.

Grant presses his palm between his eyes and suppresses a groan. "This wasn't supposed to go like this."

A family with two little girls walks out the door. Each girl has a headband with springy hearts wobbling on top, and they're dressed head to toe in pink and red. It's too much.

The laugh starts low in my chest, and then it builds until there's no holding it back. Grant looks over, horrified. I shake my head, realizing just how ridiculous this is, and grab his hand. After several moments, he cracks a smile.

"Let's get food and head back to a park or something."

He gives me a soft smile, a smile that acknowledges he knows I'm trying. "It's too cold. And dark."

I squeeze his hand. "We'll eat in the car then."

"I'm so sorry."

"Don't. It's fine." I lean closer. "We're fine."

Grant finally nods.

We get our order and find the closest well-lit, snow-covered park with street lights. Just as I'm finishing my hamburger, a glob of mustard falls from the bun and lands on my dress.

"Oh, no! Mustard is so hard to get out." I dab at my dress with a napkin. There's a half-full bottle of water tucked in the back, and I pour some onto a new napkin, hoping I can wash most of the stain out. As I scrub, little bits of brown napkin start to rub onto my dress.

"I don't think this evening is going to get any better," Grant says as I fuss over my outfit. "So I'm just going to give this to you now."

When I look up, I see he's holding a long velvet box. My heartbeat increases, and I swallow. "You already bought me flowers."

He nudges the box toward me, and I take it gingerly. When I open it, I find a simple silver necklace with a twisted pendant over a citrine, my birthstone.

"It's beautiful," I whisper, feeling like a ton of bricks has settled in my stomach.

"We haven't talked about us," Grant says, watching as I run my finger over the chain. "I kept getting the impression that you didn't want a relationship, that you wanted to keep it open." He pauses and meets my eyes. "But I like you, Lauren. Only you. I don't want to date any other girls, and I really don't want you seeing any other guys."

I blink at him, my breath catching with joy. Or panic.

I'm not sure which.

"So what do you say? Can we be exclusive?"

I nod slowly at first, and then, as I make up my mind, more confidently. "Yes."

Grant grins, and he looks relieved. He nods toward the necklace. "You want to try it on?"

He pulls the delicate chain from the box. It's beautiful—it really is. I tilt in the seat so my back is toward him and pull my hair to the side. He settles the necklace around my neck, and his fingers brush against my skin as he hooks the clasp.

I run my hand over it, telling myself it's fine. I'll get used to wearing it.

My skin already itches.

"Thank you," I murmur.

Instead of drawing back, Grant brushes his fingers against my neck. Steeling my courage, I turn. He smiles and leans in.

Grant kisses like he does everything else—with practiced skill. But the car door is hard against my back, and it's starting to get cold. I pull back first.

"I guess it's time I get you home?" he asks, obviously hoping I'll say no.

I nod.

His smile fades a little, but he sighs and starts the engine. "The next date will be better. I promise."

When we arrive at the house, the windows are black except for the one in the entry. My parents are still out.

But why wouldn't they be? It's just after nine.

I could ask Grant in, invite him to watch a movie or something, but I'm not up to it tonight.

"I'll walk you to the door." He turns off the engine.

Together, we walk up to the entry and pause by the front door. Grant slips his arms around my waist, drawing me close. Without fear of my father peering out from one of the windows, he kisses me. I wrap my arms around his neck, trying to feel something more than a dull warmth.

I like Grant, but there's no spark.

Playing with the hair at the nape of his neck, I pull him closer. There must be something here. There has to be.

Grant makes a low sound in the back of his throat, and he pulls me closer.

Suddenly, car lights shine on us as a truck pulls into the drive. Grant and I break apart. I'm sure he's worried it's my parents returning for the night, but it's worse. It's Harrison.

Harrison continues around the circle drive, disappearing behind the house. My heart beats in a mad rhythm, and I feel like I've done something horribly wrong.

But I haven't. My boyfriend was just kissing me goodnight. My boyfriend, Grant. Grant my boyfriend.

I'll get used to it eventually.

Grant leans forward and kisses me one more time, a soft goodbye peck. "I'll call you tomorrow. Maybe we can hang out after my game?"

I nod.

"You are coming to the game, aren't you?"

After hesitating for just a moment, I nod again.

He gives me that all-star smile of his. "I'll see you tomorrow afternoon then."

We say goodnight, and then I shut the door. I stand in the foyer for a moment, running my hand over my forehead.

"Your dad would have freaked out if he'd seen you."

I jump and glare at Harrison. He's standing in the entry, leaning against the wall, eating a sandwich. How did he even have time to make that? Didn't he just get here?

He takes another bite, watching me, waiting for me to say something.

"But he didn't." As soon as I hear Grant's car pull out of the drive, I unclasp the chain and drag it from my neck.

Harrison's eyes stay trained on the necklace, but he doesn't mention it. Instead, he asks, "Did you have a good night?"

I brush past him, irritated for no rational reason other than he's here, standing in my house, eating a sandwich, and looking ridiculously handsome in the jeans and button-down shirt he wore to work.

Of course, he follows me upstairs.

"Go away," I say. "I have to change."

Harrison raises an eyebrow, leans against my door frame, and takes another bite of his sandwich. "Be my guest."

He looks so devilishly handsome, I almost laugh as I push him into the hall and close the door.

"You never answered how your night was," he calls from the other side.

After I set the necklace on my vanity, I pull my dress over my head and scowl at the mustard splotch. "It was fabulous."

"It sounds like it was fabulous. You're in the best mood."

After I pull on yoga pants and a huge T-shirt, I open the door and scoot past him. "I got mustard on my dress."

Again, he follows me, this time into the laundry room. I spray the spot with stain remover and set it on the washer to soak.

"So are you guys a thing now, or what?"

I let out a slow breath. "Yeah."

Finished with his sandwich, he slides his hands into his pockets. "About time."

"Right? What was I waiting for?" I mean to say the words casually, but they end up coming out forced.

His eyes stay on mine, his expression void of emotion. It's unnerving, and I look away.

"Okay, I'm exhausted." I motion for him to move

along. "You can go now."

Harrison raises an eyebrow, his gaze still on me. "I'm dismissed, huh?"

Several beats go by before I say, "Yep."

Chapter Seventeen
April 15th

"We have to pick a theme," our student council president states. Janna peers at her clipboard. "So far we have the Roaring' Twenties, Masquerade, Paris, and...that's it. Any more ideas?"

Vance leans forward, almost tossing Kally off his lap. "What happened to Zombie Prom?

Janna gives him a withering look. "I vetoed that."

It's the prom committee's first official meeting, and I'm so brimming with ideas, I can barely contain myself. Luckily Grant has his arm draped over my shoulders, unknowingly holding me in place. He's here in payment for all the games I've been going to. Basketball ended, and baseball started soon after. It's an endless string of sports.

Prom committee is a small exchange, in my opinion.

"What about a garden theme?" I ask.

Janna looks at me. "What do you have in mind?"

I scoot forward, fully prepared. "The botanical gardens has the large outdoor amphitheater, and it's available for rent for special events. The gardens are in full bloom in mid-May, and there are lanterns and lit fountains, which would save a lot of money from our decorating budget."

"What if it rains?" Kally asks.

Honestly. Like I haven't already thought of that.

"They have a huge meeting hall. If the weather is bad, we could use that as a backup."

Janna nods. "That's not a bad idea—if they'd let us use it."

They will. I already called to check. I don't tell her because I don't want to seem too eager.

"Well, we were going to discuss venue next, but I like the idea of the botanical gardens," Janna says. "Any other ideas?"

"There's the convention center," a junior says, but she doesn't sound too excited about it.

Most of the school's proms have been there, except for the dreadful event from last year that ended up in the school's gymnasium when there was a possible gas leak at the center.

"Anyone else?" Janna asks. When no one answers, she turns to me. "Lauren, do you want to give them a

186

call? Check on prices and availability?"

"Sure." I say it like it's no big deal, but inside I'm dancing. I've wanted to do prom at the gardens since I was a freshman. I have no idea why no one has thought of it before.

"That's enough for today," Janna says. "We'll meet again next Friday at the same time."

Grant grins. "I have baseball practice after school next Friday."

He doesn't have to look so happy about it. I elbow him in the ribs, and he laughs.

Janna rolls her eyes. "You're only here because we need Lauren, so I think we'll get along just fine without you."

Grant clutches his chest. "That hurts."

The room laughs adoringly at their golden boy, and I only shake my head, used to it. It's a little weird, like dating a boy version of Riley. Except Riley and I have things like fashion and hair and makeup in common. Believe it or not, Grant's not at all interested in discussing those things.

We walk from the classroom, and Grant laces his fingers in mine. We turn the corner, and, seeing that the hall is empty, he wraps his arms around my waist. His thumbs hook into the loop at the back of my jeans, and he brushes a kiss to my lips.

"When does your practice start?" I interrupt.

He checks his watch. "Fifteen minutes."

When he leans in to kiss me again, Janna turns the corner. With an irritated smile, he pulls back.

"A group of us are going to the movies tonight," she says. "You guys should come."

Grant looks at me, letting me decide.

"Sure," I answer even though I've gotten behind on my blog with all the games I've been going to lately.

Janna tosses her hair over her shoulder. "Invite Riley, too."

We discuss it for a few more moments, and then Grant walks me to my car.

"I'll pick you up at six thirty," he promises.

When I get to my house, Riley's car is already in the drive. I find her in the kitchen with Harrison.

"You're early," I say to her as I help myself to a bowl of berries Mom has on the counter.

Riley shrugs. "I didn't have anything to do after school, so I came over here."

Even though she knew I'd be late today.

Interesting.

She's sitting next to Harrison, watching him do something on his laptop.

They look rather cozy.

"For work or for school?" I ask Harrison.

He always seems to be working on something these days.

"School," he answers.

I turn from them and rummage through a cupboard, looking for a glass. "We're going to the movies tonight," I say to Riley. "Janna wanted me to invite you."

"She wanted you to invite me?" There's a teasing tone in Harrison's voice. "That's nice of her."

After I find a glass, I turn around and give him a look. "*Riley*, Janna wanted me to invite you."

"You should come!" Riley slides her hand over Harrison's arm.

My eyes follow her fingers as they brush from his elbow to his wrist.

"I have to finish this, and then I have a project for work." Harrison's eyes never leave the screen.

"That's all you've been doing since I got here," Riley pouts. "Surely you can take a few hours off?"

I thought Riley was over Harrison. She hasn't mentioned him in forever.

Maybe she just can't stand to have a boy not fall at her feet and look at her adoringly.

Or she's just a sucker for his greenish-blue eyes and the way he always smells faintly of quality aftershave. Or perhaps it's the way his lips are perfectly shaped, his top lip a sculpted bow...

I blink away my thoughts, not liking the direction they're traveling.

I've been dating Grant for over two months now, and absolutely nothing has happened between me and Harrison. Our relationship has shifted to purely platonic. It's no different than having Brandon back in the house. Except nicer, because Harrison's in the guest house and not in the next room.

That would be awkward.

"We'll have so much fun!" Riley says, her eyes bright as she continues to trail her hand up and down Harrison's arm.

Whoa. What did I miss?

Harrison only nods, a polite smile on his face. His eyes shift to me, and then his smile becomes wary. "You don't mind if I come, do you, Lauren?"

"Of course not."

Will Grant mind? Maybe.

He and Harrison still haven't fully clicked. They're polite. But neither of them go out of their way to be overly friendly.

"How was prom planning?" Riley asks.

Happy to change the subject, I lean on the counter. "Janna liked my idea to use the botanical gardens. She asked me to call them for information."

Riley raises an eyebrow. "Didn't you already do that?"

"Yes, but I didn't want to seem overly zealous."

She sits back, finally letting her hand stray from

Harrison's arm. "You're not too zealous—you're efficient."

"Well, they don't need to know just how efficient I am."

Harrison murmurs an acknowledgment. "Don't want to threaten those in charge. You'll end up being the one blowing up balloons an hour before the dance."

I shudder at the thought of missing my salon appointment. That would definitely put a strain on the day.

We hang out in the kitchen for several hours, mostly because Harrison's still in here. It's obvious that Riley has no intention of leaving.

Grant shows up right on time, and I usher him in. He greets Riley with a big smile and acknowledges Harrison with a nod.

The atmosphere becomes slightly strained.

"Should we all take the same car?" Riley asks when it's time to walk out the door.

Both Harrison and Grant pause, obviously not keen on the idea.

"Why don't you and Harrison take his car, and I'll ride with Grant," I offer.

Harrison shoots me a look. Apparently he's even less keen on that idea.

Well, too bad. He's the one that said yes.

"Does Riley still have a thing for Harrison?" Grant

asks as we pull out of the neighborhood.

I glance in the side mirror at the truck behind us. "She did. I thought she was over it."

Grant doesn't respond. Not wanting to talk about Harrison and Riley, I change the subject. By the time we reach the theater, I've distracted him by bringing up his last game.

We get to the theater before the rest of the group, and we stand to the side, trying to decide what movie we should see. Just before it's time for several to start, Janna and a few of her friends show up.

"I just don't see what the point of a movie is if something doesn't explode," Grant argues, grinning.

Riley rolls her eyes. "Something might explode in The Love Letter Diaries."

Grant looks disgusted, and Riley laughs. I stay out of it. I browsed the listings, and there is nothing I want to watch. Tonight, I guess I'm here for the popcorn.

"Let's take a vote," Janna says.

"No," Grant argues, noting the guys are outnumbered three to five. "Let's flip a coin."

Harrison digs a quarter out of his pocket.

"Tails," Grant calls.

The coin lands heads up, and Grant looks at Harrison like it's his fault.

"Sorry." Harrison laughs and holds his hand up in surrender.

We buy our tickets and filter into the theater. I'm directly behind Riley, but Harrison pauses at the aisle. Being a gentleman, he allows her to go in first. I hesitate but then follow him in. What else can I do?

About an hour into the movie—which ends up being about a woman who grew up in love with her brother's best friend—I realize I should have done everything in my power to make sure I wasn't smack-dab between Harrison and my boyfriend.

They're both bored, and because of it, they're restless. Harrison accidentally brushes his elbow next to my arm as he takes a drink of his soda. Grant shifts in his seat and his leg presses against mine.

I sit like a statue, trying very hard not to breathe Harrison in—trying not to feel too self-conscious about Grant's hand resting just above my knee.

When the movie finally ends—and I do mean finally; it was easily three hours long—I jump up as soon as the credits begin to roll.

"It's almost eleven." Grant frowns at his watch.

I pull his arm down, almost not believing him. "I have to be home in eight minutes."

He blows out a slow breath. "So do I."

Grant's an only child, and his parents are almost as protective as mine. Both sets are going to freak out if we're home after eleven, and we'll get the royal inquisition about what exactly it was we were doing.

"Lauren can ride back with us," Riley offers.

The look that flashes across Grant's face is not a happy one, but he knows it's the solution that makes the most sense.

"Okay," he finally says. Before we part in the parking lot, he pulls me into a kiss.

My cheeks grow hot when he lingers for longer than is socially acceptable. I break away as soon as possible and pat him on the arm. "I'll see you tomorrow."

Riley whistles low when we get into Harrison's truck. "What was that?"

I crawl to the backseat and brush a stray hair out of my face. "What was what?"

Harrison starts the truck, not saying a word.

"That was a "going-off-to-war" kiss, not an "I'll-see-you-tomorrow-at-my-baseball-game" kiss."

I fidget with my purse strap and roll my eyes. There's no way I'm answering that one.

"You couldn't have possibly liked that movie," Harrison says, changing the subject after a long and uncomfortable lull in the conversation.

"It was awful," I agree.

Riley glares at us. "It was *beautiful*. What's wrong with the two of you?"

Harrison grins. "It was painful."

"It was long," I add.

"She died in the end," he says.

I meet his gaze in the rearview mirror. "*I* wanted to die in the end."

We end up laughing, and Riley pouts. "You two wouldn't know art if it bit you on the nose."

"That was art?" I snort and start to laugh harder.

"You obviously have bad taste," Riley says to Harrison, ignoring me. "What's your favorite movie?"

Without hesitating, he gives her the title of a comedy that was so ridiculous—so absurd—it was absolutely wonderful.

I lean forward. "I love that movie!"

Riley rolls her eyes, truly disgusted. "You also have horrible taste."

When we get to the house, Riley waves a goodbye and heads straight to her car. I'm five minutes late when Harrison and I end up walking through the door, but it doesn't matter because my parents aren't home.

A twinge of unease settles in my stomach.

They didn't mention going out tonight.

"Where are they?" I ask Harrison, hoping he'll know.

"Check your phone."

I pull it out of my purse, and sure enough, there's a missed text.

"They went over to Dad's coworker's house for dinner," I tell him. "But Mom said they'd be home by ten-thirty."

I glance at the grandfather clock in the entry. It's now six minutes after eleven.

They're never late. Not ever.

"I'm sure it's fine," Harrison says, picking up on my worry. "Just call her."

The call goes straight to Mom's voice mail. Immediately, I call Dad's number. As the call goes through, a melodic chime starts upstairs. Frustrated, I type a quick text to my Mom, asking her to call me.

Worried, I drum my fingers on my hip.

"You know what?" Harrison says. "I'm not tired. How about we watch a movie? Something better than what we just sat through."

Without waiting for my answer, he walks into the living room and finds the remote. I sit in the recliner and watch him scroll through the options.

Why hasn't she called? It's not like her to forget.

Harrison ends up picking a romantic comedy that would normally make me laugh, but tonight, my mind is elsewhere. At eleven forty-five, I try to call again.

By midnight, I'm a nervous wreck.

Harrison has been shooting covert, worried glances at me since the movie started, but, this time, he frowns and hits pause. "I'm sure it's fine."

But he doesn't mean it anymore. He's worried too.

"Someone would call me, right?" My throat feels thick. "If something happened, someone would know to call?"

He kneels in front of me. "Sure. They'd check the numbers in your mom's phone."

But Mom's phone is dead.

Did she forget to charge it? Or did something happen to it...

"Lauren." Harrison's voice is low and careful. "We don't know that something is wrong. You need to take a breath and try to calm down."

My mind keeps running wild with all the horrible things that could have happened to them. Tears start to prick my eyes. They're never late.

Never, never.

Harrison pulls me up and wraps me in his arms. He rests his cheek on my head, and his hands run slowly over my back in an attempt to soothe me.

And then my phone rings.

I jump back, scrambling to answer the call. It's an unknown number. Fear shoots through me, real this time. No one calls after midnight unless it's an emergency. I stare at it, too terrified to answer.

Harrison takes the phone from my hand.

"Hello?" His voice is tight, and then his face washes with relief. "Hi, Deb, yeah it's Harrison...She was worried, so I stayed with her...No, she's fine."

My stomach clenches, and my hands tremble with relief.

He hands me the phone.

"Mom? What happened?"

"We're fine, honey. We were in an accident on the way home."

It's all my worst fears realized, but she says they're okay, so I can breathe.

"My phone died while we were at Roy and Tanya's house, and I couldn't get ahold of you," she continues. "I'm calling from the hospital now. Dad's waiting to see a doctor."

"What's wrong with him?"

"He hit the window pretty hard, and he's having some shoulder pain. The paramedics didn't seem too worried, but they said we needed to come in."

I sit in the recliner, my legs about to go out. "When will you be home?"

"A few hours at least. It's the emergency room, so who knows? Are you okay?"

"Harrison's here."

"I'm so sorry, Lauren. I didn't mean to scare you."

My chin starts to quiver, more because I'm so relieved that they're okay. "I'm all right."

"We'll be home after a while, okay? Don't worry anymore. We're fine."

I stay brave until I hang up, and then I bury

my head in my hands and choke back a sob. Again, Harrison pulls me into his arms. I burrow against him, letting him comfort me.

This time, he leads me over to the couch and pulls me down with him.

"Look what I found," he says.

There, on the screen, is the movie we talked about on the way home.

"Do you want to watch it?" he asks.

I nod, and he rubs my shoulder a moment longer before he sits back, giving me space. I pull a throw from the back of the couch, wrap it around my legs, and settle an appropriate distance away. But the whole time we watch the movie, I wish we were just a little closer.

Chapter Eighteen
May 6th

I carefully unroll a section of ivory sequined material from the bolt and measure it with a yardstick. It glitters in the auditorium lights, shimmering in a subdued, classy way. I can't wait to see it layered on the white tablecloth-covered tables in the arboretum garden.

Sitting back on my heels, I admire the stack I've finished. I only have five more left, and then we'll use the remainder for the refreshment tables.

Janna had originally hoped to use a cheaper muslin for the table covers, but we saved enough with the decorations by booking the botanical gardens that we were able to afford the more expensive sequins. That, and this material won't fray. Good thing it doesn't because it's a pain to sew.

Footsteps echo from behind me, but I'm too busy cutting to turn around. Hands settle on my shoulders, and then Grant leans down for a kiss. Distracted, I give him a peck and continue my work.

"How much longer are you going to be?" he asks.

I finish the cut and set my scissors aside. "Five minutes? Ten, maybe?"

"You said that fifteen minutes ago."

Stretching, I stand up. "I'm sorry. The fabric gums up the scissors, and it's taking longer than I expected. You can go. I'll just have my mom pick me up."

Grant lets out a slow sigh. "You mean Harrison."

I set my hands on my hips. "No, I mean my mom."

"I'm sorry, I just..." He runs a hand over his face. "Never mind."

I've been nothing but faithful to Grant. Yes, it's possible I'm still drawn to Harrison. I still feel a flutter around him. But I've kept my distance, given almost all of my time to Grant. Between prom and going to Grant's games, I haven't even posted anything other than a quick, "I'm-busy-but-I-swear-I'll-be-back" post to my blog for over two weeks. The reason this has taken so long is because I was snapping pictures of my project with my phone for later. Even if I don't do a video, I can write up a simple post.

Trying to ease Grant's nerves, I say, "Listen—I'm one of Harrison's best friend's little sisters. He's a little protective...he's kind of a brat."

He stares at a point in the auditorium, shaking

his head.

I set my hand on Grant's arm, drawing his attention back to me. In the three months we've dated, I've come to truly care about him. He's my friend, a good friend. He's sweet and kind, and I know he really cares about me. I don't want him dwelling on things that were never meant to be.

When his gaze travels back to me, I gently place my hands on his cheeks and kiss him. "I'll finish this at home."

I'm not sure where I'll find enough room to work on it, but I'll figure that out later.

Grant's face softens, and he kisses me back. "There's a party at Daniel's house tonight. I told him we'd drop by."

My stomach knots with nerves. I don't do parties—Grant knows that. There's nothing worse than the stale smell of too many bodies and the high-pitched giggles of random girls trying to impress the jocks. I haven't been to a party since my sophomore year when Riley was curious. We left fifteen minutes after we got there, and we've never been to another one.

He gives me a look. "We'll just drop by."

"Or we could not."

Grant runs a hand over my arm. "I know it's not your thing, but these are my friends. I can't keep blowing them off."

Part of me is scared to see Grant at a party. Sure, he's all "boy-next-door" here in school, but what's he like there? What if he's different?

"Okay," I say slowly, already dreading it.

Grant hugs me. "It will be fun."

I murmur an acknowledgment against his muscular chest.

After I gather my material, I follow Grant to his car. He drove me this morning, as he does most days now. My car barely leaves the driveway anymore.

"I'll pick you up in a few hours, okay?" Grant says as I slip out of the car.

I nod, distracted. The day is warm, and the sun feels good on my shoulders. The tulips have finished blooming for the season, but the daffodils are still going strong. I should clip a few from the back of the bed and bring them into the kitchen.

Grant doesn't leave, and when I glance back, he looks uncertain.

"Lauren?" he asks.

Leaning down, I take a closer look at the flowers. "Yeah?"

He looks nervous, which just makes me nervous. "You could wear something a little more casual."

I glance down at my skinny jeans, heels, and sleeveless blouse. I look great if I do say so myself. What does he want me to wear? A T-shirt?

As if reading the indignation on my face, he holds up a placating hand. "No, sweetheart, you look awesome. That's not what I mean."

I set a hand on my hip. "What exactly do you mean then?"

Grant looks like he's regretting opening his mouth. "We'll probably be in the backyard. People will be playing volleyball and stuff, and you look a little…"

"Stuffy?"

"I don't want your outfit to get ruined, that's all."

What exactly am I getting myself into that my outfit could be ruined?

"Okay."

He tilts his head, giving me a puppy-dog look. "Are you mad?"

"Of course not." I take a slow breath through my nose and work up a smile. "An outfit must match the occasion, right?"

"I know you're irritated, but I appreciate that you're trying."

I want to tell him that he's trying too, but I doubt he would understand my meaning.

"I'll see you soon, okay?"

I nod then watch him leave the yard. He waves out the window as he pulls from the drive. Still miffed, I toss open the front door and then shut it with slightly more enthusiasm than necessary.

"Bad day?" Harrison asks from the living room.

I eye him. "Don't you have a couch in the guest house?"

That slow smile builds at the edges of his mouth, and he doesn't take his eyes off his laptop screen. "Sure, but the house is so much cozier, don't you think?"

I roll my eyes.

"What's ruffled your feathers?"

Ignoring his teasing, I motion to my outfit. "How do I look?"

He looks up, and his expression instantly goes guarded, as if he's worried the question is a trap. "You look fine...why?"

"Fine?"

Sighing, he shuts his laptop. His tone careful, he says, "You look amazing, Lauren. You always look amazing—you always know you look amazing. What stupid thing did Grant say this time?"

I huff out a breath and toss my backpack on the couch. "Nothing. He just wanted me to change before he drags me to some dumb party one of his jock friends is throwing."

Harrison shakes his head and opens the laptop back up. His eyes on the screen, he says, "You don't belong at one of those parties."

My hackles instantly rise. "Excuse me?"

Harrison looks back up. "You actually want to go?"

"Well, of course not. But that doesn't mean I don't *belong* there.*"

He stands, and his expression makes me wonder if he's as irritated with me as I was with Grant. Laptop tucked under his arm, he takes the two steps toward me. "You really want my opinion?"

I motion for him to continue.

"You're too mature to get sucked into that world."

"Really? Because the day you set foot in this house you said I wasn't mature enough to admit"—I make quotes with my fingers— "that I was in love with you."

He steps closer, too close. "I was trying to get a rise out of you, and you know it."

"And why would you do that?"

He shifts a little closer. "You know why."

My pulse quickens, and I lick my lips. "Why don't you explain anyway?"

The front door opens and shuts and Mom hollers, "Come help me with these grocery bags!"

Harrison takes a step back, an enigmatic look on his face. He tilts his head to the side, raises his brows, and then turns toward the foyer.

My heart hammers in my chest, making me feel lightheaded.

"When do you leave for your cousin's wedding?" Mom asks Harrison when we reach the kitchen.

"On the twentieth," he answers.

Mom glances at the calendar. "That's the day before prom, isn't it, Lauren?" She laughs and turns back to Harrison, teasing. "I guess we won't be sending you as Lauren and Grant's chaperone then."

My eyes fly to Harrison, but his full attention is on a mesh bag of oranges.

Mom chatters as we finish helping her put things away, and I escape to my bedroom as soon as I get the chance.

What, exactly, is one supposed to wear to a backyard party? I keep my jeans on because the late May evening will not be warm enough for a summer skirt, but I exchange my heels for flats. I also grab a long, lightweight white cardigan that I just found at the mall last weekend. It's super cute.

I glance at my blouse. What's wrong with it? It's not too dressy. After all, I wore it to school.

In the end, I pull my hair up in a loose ponytail and call it good. I changed out of my heels. What else could Grant want?

I watch for my boyfriend, and when he pulls up, I leave without waiting for him to come to the door. I'm not excited about the night, and I have a feeling my parents will like it even less. Guilt churns in my stomach, but I won't do anything stupid, so it will be all fine. Tedious, but fine.

Grant's eyes wander over my outfit. "You didn't

really change."

"Yes, I did." I point to my feet. "I was in heels."

He doesn't say anything. He doesn't even roll his eyes—but it looks like he wants to. The drive is slightly strained. Why does he care so much about what I wear?

Twenty minutes later, I find out "casual" is obviously code for "less fabric." Despite that it's going to be a cool night, several girls are in short shorts and skimpy tank-tops. They have to be freezing. I can see how Grant would be embarrassed by his fully-clothed girlfriend.

Unable to keep my mouth shut, I tell him as much, hissing the words under my breath.

"That's not it," Grant argues. "I was just hoping you could wear something that makes you look a little less unapproachable."

"I'm not unapproachable," I say.

"Sweetheart," Grant says. "You are the most unapproachable person I know."

I blink at him, hurt.

He takes my hand and pulls me farther into the party. "Let's forget it. There's no reason to fight."

Holding Grant's hand, I fake a smile, trying to look "approachable," as we make our way through the throng of people. Daniel yells a greeting across the backyard, and Grant acknowledges him.

A few of Riley's cheerleader friends are here, and

they say hi, but most everyone else ignores me. I'm just Grant's arm decoration—and apparently a poor decoration at that.

The sun sets, and a chill tinges the spring night air. One of the girls next to me shivers when a breeze blows through, and I bite back a smile as she wraps her bare arms around herself, obviously cold.

I'm perfectly comfortable.

A rowdy group shows up, hollering as they step out the back door. And they've bought refreshments. Soon the party gets a little too wild for my tastes.

"Can we go?"

Grant looks torn, obviously not wanting to leave this early. "Just a little longer?"

A headache is blooming behind my left eye. I have fabric to cut, and I simply don't want to be here. "I'd rather go now."

"You can't leave, dude," Daniel says, overhearing us. "The party is just getting started!"

Despite me sitting right here, a girl from one of the neighboring schools leans over Grant's shoulder. "Come on, Grant. You can't leave now." She flashes me a vicious smirk, and then she purrs in his ear, "Remember how much fun we had at that party last summer?"

And that's my cue.

I stand, letting Grant decide whether or not he's

going to follow me. I don't care at this point. If he doesn't want to leave, I'll call Riley. She'll come pick me up—she'll give me grief for being here—but she'd come get me.

Apparently, I don't have to worry about it, though. Grant excuses himself and follows me out.

"Sorry about that," he murmurs as he wraps his arm around my waist.

I stop. "For the party or for the girl?"

He takes a breath. "Both, I guess. I knew you would hate it. I shouldn't have dragged you here."

There's something in his voice that makes me pause. I study him, the curve of his shoulders, the angle of his chin.

We're not doing as well as I had thought. I had hoped it was just me.

"Come on," he says, sliding his hand to catch mine in his palm. "Let's get you home."

Grant didn't stay after he dropped me off—not that I expected him to. I didn't ask what he was going to do with the rest of his evening, either. He may have gone back to the party for all I know.

Now I'm sitting in the kitchen, brooding over it.

Dad winces as he reaches into the top cabinet for the jar of cinnamon. Ignoring the pain, he pulls the spice down and continues gathering ingredients. He's making a pear crisp—his own recipe.

"How's your shoulder?" I hop up to grab the flour and brown sugar from another cabinet so he doesn't have to pull it out too.

Dad sets the cinnamon on the counter and rotates his arm a few times. "It's still pretty messed up."

It still hasn't healed after the accident.

"When do we go to Missoula?"

He has to see a doctor there, someone who specializes in shoulder injuries.

Distracted, he says, "In a few weeks."

Mom walks into the kitchen, sees Dad rubbing his arm, and frowns. "We'll be going the second to last weekend in May. I was thinking we'd make a weekend of it, maybe all of us go see a show? It'll be nice to spend some time with Brandon."

What weekend is that?

Realizing when it is, I say, "Mom, prom is that Saturday."

We just talked about it this afternoon. How could she forget?

Her face falls as she glances at the calendar on the fridge. "Oh, I didn't even think about it being the same weekend. I forgot to write it in my planner."

"It's okay," I assure her. "I can probably stay with Riley. Or, I'm eighteen...I could stay here..."

Both my parents look up, staring at me blankly.

"By yourself?" Dad asks.

I roll my eyes. "Yes, by myself."

They exchange a look, and I'm getting ready to argue. Technically, I could move out if I wanted to. Technically, I could get married if I wanted to.

Suddenly, the worry in Dad's expression eases from his face. "Harrison would be just out back if you need anything." He shrugs and winces again. "I guess it's fine."

"Harrison has a wedding in Connecticut that weekend," Mom says.

That she remembers.

"Oh." Dad's forehead wrinkles. "Well, I guess it's all right if you're here alone...but why don't you see if you can stay with Riley? Or Grandma and Grandpa?"

After a quick phone call, it's all arranged.

I guess I'm staying at Riley's.

Chapter Nineteen
May 20th

"No, they were supposed to be coral peonies." I tap my foot on my bedroom rug. "Not pink."

The woman on the phone assures me that they are a very salmony pink.

The entire color scheme will be off, and it's my fault. I was the one who insisted on fresh flowers for the table decorations. But how can you do a garden party theme without fresh flowers?

Janna's going to be ticked. She wanted to order the cardboard centerpieces.

I rub my throbbing temples. I can fix this. Somehow, I can make it work. It's not like prom is tomorrow or anything.

Oh my, prom *is* tomorrow.

"It's fine," I say into the phone. "I'll pick them up in the morning at nine."

My mind whirls madly. How am I going to integrate pink into our theme? What can I add to the bouquets?

My eyes land on the vase of crepe paper flowers on my vanity.

It could work.

It has to work.

I'm only fifteen minutes late getting to the school where the prom committee has agreed to meet to put together the rest of the decorations for tomorrow.

I arrive with a bag full of crepe paper, floral wire, and eight glue guns.

"I'm so sorry," I call out as I push the gymnasium doors open. "We had a mix-up with the—"

My words die in my throat as I survey the group, which consists of Janna.

Only Janna.

"Where is everyone?" I ask.

"Dylan and Hannah are sick," she says. "I have no idea where Vance and Kally are..."

Not good. Not good.

One by one, she lists everyone else in the committee, and she finally says, "Where's Grant?"

"He has an out of town baseball game at three."

His team is already on their way to the next town, and I'm supposed to drive over just as soon as I'm done here.

And there is no way I'm going to make it because I have four-hundred coral and light pink crepe paper peonies to make.

Janna looks stressed, and she's surrounded by about a billion balloons for the tacky arch I tried to talk her out of. "We're never going to get this done on our own."

"Don't say that." My finger twitches against the plastic bag. "We have to get it done."

I dig for my phone as I toss my bag on the floor. Riley answers on the second ring. Her brothers squeal in the background, and she sounds frazzled.

"Can you come help us with the prom decorations?" I ask in lieu of a greeting. "No one showed up."

"I'm babysitting my brothers," she says. "And I can't bring them. They're tiny tornadoes."

She's right. They'd trail behind us, destroying everything we put together.

"Did you try Grant?" she asks.

"He's going to an out of town baseball game."

She goes through more people, but half of them were supposed to be here to begin with. I only start to panic once I hang up.

Janna's wrestling with the balloons, fighting with the arch.

"Shouldn't we be making that tomorrow?" I ask.

She looks flustered. "I thought it would be better to make it now and take it in the back of Brady's van."

"Will it fit?"

The student council president blows a strand of hair out of her face. "I have no idea."

I watch her for a few minutes more, thinking. I'm about to get started on the paper peonies when my phone rings.

I really don't have time to deal with Harrison right now.

"Yeah?" I ask, my voice curt.

"I can't find my tablet," Harrison says. "Have you seen it?"

"You left it on the end table."

He mutters something, and then he says, "It's not here."

"The one with the lamp."

"Oh...oh, yeah. I see it. Thanks."

I'm about to hang up when he says, "What are you doing?"

"Freaking out."

He laughs. "What about?"

I tell him our dilemma and then say, "I don't know how we're going to finish it all."

There's a long pause. "I have to be at the airport at five...but I guess I could help."

Startled, I look at my phone. "With prom

decorations?"

Isn't that exactly the kind of thing he was hoping to avoid?

"Sure. I'm already packed. I'll head to the high school right now."

"Okay, um, thanks."

Janna looks up when I end the call. "Who was that?"

I scoot next to the wall, dragging my bag with me. "That was help. And he's on his way."

It only takes fifteen minutes for Harrison to make it. Janna's jaw goes a little slack when he walks through the door, looking all teen-movie hot. Seeing him again, newly through Janna's eyes, makes my pulse jump a little too.

"Hey," he says to Janna, and then he squats down next to me. "I'm all yours. Do with me what you will."

Four hours and fifty-six minutes after Harrison walks through the door, we have finished the paper peonies, a chalkboard welcome sign, one balloon arch, the band backdrop, and the photo booth extras. I've burned my fingers with hot glue more times than I can count, and I've broken not one, but two nails.

Thankfully, I have an appointment to have them done tomorrow morning.

Janna had to leave, and now it's just me and Harrison, trying to beat the clock. He has to be at the airport in a little less than an hour.

We're painting the lattice-work archway a deep coral color (the same color the peonies were supposed to be). It's quickly becoming apparent that, though he's a better woodworker, I am far more skilled with a paintbrush.

"You have a drip," I say, motioning to the runny wet splotch with my own brush.

Harrison peers at the spot and tries to even it out, but he still has too much paint on his brush. I step between him and the archway and smooth the drip.

"I was going to fix it," he says.

I realize my mistake as soon as I feel the breath of his words on my neck. We're too close.

Too close.

Swiping my brush over the wood, I dart away as quickly as I can.

He doesn't mention it, but I'm sure he noticed how I fled. We continue to paint in near silence.

Once finished, I cross my arms, surveying our work. "Not bad."

Harrison stands next to me, mimicking my posture, his paintbrush still in his hand. "Not bad? I think we're pretty awesome."

As he says the words, he bumps his shoulder into

mine. I jump, startled by the contact, and accidentally step right into his paintbrush. It leaves a thick, coral smudge just below my elbow.

Harrison takes a step back and holds up his hands, paintbrush and all, in surrender. "I didn't do that. You walked into it."

I stare at the smudge, and then I look at him, determined.

He takes another step back. "Oh, no, no—I have to be on a plane in an hour."

Grinning, I take another step forward as he retreats.

Looking down as he reaches the end of the canvas drop fabric, he holds his paintbrush out like a sword. A small smile spreads across his face, lighting his eyes. "If you take a step closer, I will be forced to retaliate."

I'm about to lunge for him when a voice of reason whispers in my ear. Grant wouldn't like this.

With a sigh, I lower my paintbrush.

It only takes Harrison a moment to spot my weakness. He darts forward, pinning my arms with his own, and he holds the brush threateningly over my cheek while I squirm.

"Do you surrender?" His voice is full of good humor.

I want to say "never" and play this out, see where it will go. Instead, I sag in his arms. "Yes, fine. You win."

Slowly, he releases his grip on me. Then, just as I'm stepping away, he swipes the brush across the back of my neck.

I squeal and whip around. When I lunge at him, he grabs me in his arms, holding me tight so I can't move my brush. Our eyes meet, and we both freeze. I can feel the breath hitch in his chest.

My eyes slowly slide from his eyes to his shoulder. The moment is too much.

Harrison knows it too.

Just as he's loosening the grip on me so I can step back, the gymnasium door swings open. We jump the rest of the way apart, Harrison looking as guilty as I feel.

Riley stands there, staring at us. Her cheeks turn pink, and she looks at the ground. "I thought you needed help, so I…"

She looks at me, her face twisting in hurt.

"Riley—"

"It looks like you're pretty much done, though." Her gaze falls to the decorations we've been working on. "I'm going to go…"

She turns on her heel and rushes out the door.

Harrison sets his paintbrush down and runs a hand through his hair, looking uncomfortable. "I'm sorry. I shouldn't have—"

"I'll call her as soon as I'm done here," I interrupt.

He nods. "I need to get to the airport anyway."

I collect the painting supplies, getting ready to wash them out. "When's the wedding?"

"Tomorrow morning."

I raise an eyebrow. "Cutting it a little close, aren't you?"

"It was hard taking time off of work as it was," he answers. "It would have been impossible to stay there longer."

"When are you coming back?"

"The day after tomorrow."

It's good he'll be gone tomorrow. It would be too awkward, him seeing you in your prom dress. You waiting for his reaction when it's Grant's that's supposed to matter.

"Thanks for helping," I say, striving for normal. "I hope you have a good flight."

He shoves his hands in his pockets, just as I expect him to do—just as he does every time things become a little too tense between us. "You're welcome."

Another silence settles, and both of us try not to look at each other.

Finally, after exchanging an awkward goodbye, he leaves.

As soon as he's out the door, I crumple to the floor. I've hurt Riley, and though nothing happened, I feel guilty.

But I was stepping back—so was he. We knew we

stepped out of bounds, and we were fixing it.

We were.

But neither of us wanted to.

I rub the back of my neck, trying to work out the tension. And that's how Riley finds me. Apparently, she didn't leave after all.

Without a word, she settles to the floor, the picture of limber grace.

"Hey." I don't meet her eyes.

"Hey."

I stare at the drying paint in the tray. It's going to be such a pain to clean up now.

"You could have told me you liked him," Riley says.

Sure, I could deny it. But what's the point? It would be a lie.

"If it helps, I really tried not to like him." I inspect one of my broken fingernails. "I should have told you."

She sighs and leans back on her palms. "Honestly? I already knew. Everyone knew. Good grief, even Grant knew, but he didn't want to admit it to himself."

Feeling miserable, I sink into myself.

"He has it so bad for you."

I look up, peering at her from under the long bangs that have escaped my ponytail. "Grant?"

Obviously not mad, she stretches her legs out. "Harrison. He's absolutely head over heels in love with you. Everyone knows that, too."

My heart warms, but then I'm hit with another wave of guilt.

"You think so?"

She smirks, looking like the cat who ate the canary. "Of course I do. Why else wouldn't he want me?"

I roll my eyes.

Suddenly, she sits straight up and looks at the clock on the wall. "Lauren! Weren't you supposed to be at Grant's game two hours ago?"

I go cold, and a hard knot forms in my stomach. "I forgot."

This is bad, bad, bad. I didn't even call him.

I drop my hands to my lap and place my forehead on my clasped palms. "No one showed up, and I had a bunch of paper flowers to make…"

"He'll forgive you." She sounds like she really believes it, too.

I'm not so sure.

Chapter Twenty
May 21st

The weather is perfect for an outdoor dance. It's growing hot today, the warmest day we've had this spring, and the evening is supposed to be in the seventies and clear. The gardens are in full bloom, and I realize I was silly to have worried so much about the pink peonies clashing. We're surrounded by all colors of flowers. Mine would have fit in no matter what color they were.

However, the coral and light pink paper flowers interspersed in the arrangements are absolutely beautiful, if I do say so myself. All the centerpieces are sitting inside the visitor's center, waiting until this afternoon to be put out. I can't wait to see them with the ivory sequined tablecloths.

The band has come early to check out their space for the evening, and Janna is speaking with them now, going over her checklist.

I've just finished attaching the balloons and paper flowers around our welcome sign, and I wander over to supervise the decorations on the lattice arbor. They've attached the balloon arch to it, and I have to say it looks festive and not at all tacky, as I had originally feared.

Kally is draping wreaths over the streetlight-style garden lights, and several other students are decorating the perimeter of the area with tulle.

Everything is going exactly as planned, which is good because my nail and hair appointment is in thirty minutes.

I wander over to Janna, who's now finished speaking with the band. "Is there anything else you want me to do before I go?"

She looks at her checklist and clicks her tongue as she reads over the items. "Archway, centerpieces, concession table...I think we're good."

"I'll be back at six to dress the tables."

"Everything looks amazing, Lauren. You're really good at this."

"Thank you," I say modestly. "It was a group effort."

I survey the area. Even though a great deal of the ideas were mine, there would be no way I could pull this all together by myself.

Janna's eyes shift behind me, and her eyes light. "Hey, Grant. I didn't think you were going to make it this morning."

I freeze. He said he wasn't coming. I bite my lip, terrified to face him. He wasn't happy with me last night when we talked on the phone.

"I need to borrow Lauren for a bit," he says.

"I'm done for now." I turn but try not to meet his eyes.

Janna's gaze flickers between us, and I'm sure she can tell something is off. "See you tonight, Lauren."

Grant motions to a nearby pathway that winds through the garden. "You want to go for a walk?"

I'm going to be late for my appointment if I don't leave now, but something tells me it's best not to mention it.

"Sure."

Grant takes my hand, but it feels wrong. I grow nervous as we leave the others behind. When we reach a secluded area, he leads me to a bench.

It feels like a romantic hideaway, a garden room hidden just for us. Roses bloom on well-tended bushes, and birds twitter from the dappled branches of the trees.

I sit, nervous, and Grant joins me.

He turns my hands over in his, lightly brushing my palms with his thumbs. "Lauren, I've been doing a lot—"

"If this is about yesterday," I interrupt. "You have to know how very sorry I am. Nothing went right—"

"It's not yesterday." Then his expression turns wry. "Well, not just yesterday."

He's breaking up with me. Prom is less than eight hours away, and *he's breaking up with me.*

I suck in a shaky breath, already feeling the mortified tears glisten in my eyes.

Grant looks down at our clasped hands. "I like you, Lauren. I probably like you too much, in fact. But I'm not sure I like *us.*"

Blinking back tears before he sees them, I say, "What do you mean?"

He looks up, meeting my gaze. "You hate coming to my games. You don't like my friends. We never seem to have anything to talk about."

I, too, look down at our hands. He's right about all those things.

Grant continues, "And I love that you love beautiful things—and I love that you're beautiful—but sometimes...sometimes I wish you'd just let it go. Wear your hair in a knot. Put on a pair of sneakers."

I wait for him to say the words, for him to end it. My heart clenches, and it hurts. It really hurts. I like Grant. I like him so much...but deep down, I know that everything he's saying is true.

227

He looks up and waits for me to meet his eyes.

"Despite all that," he says, his voice quiet, "I think we could still work. If you want it to work."

I wait for him to finish, unsure what to say, unsure what he wants me to say.

He waits for a beat, and then he squeezes my hands. "Do we want it to work? Or should we call it a game and part as friends?"

It's the sports analogy that does me in. It's not that there's anything wrong with it, but it makes his point like nothing else could.

"You're right. We're not good together," I say. "But it hurts...I don't want to let you go."

Grant lets out a long, slow sigh. He squeezes my hand. "Me either. I really do like you, Lauren."

"You won't hate me, will you?" The tears spill over even though I try to hold them back. "I...I can't imagine the thought of you hating me."

Grant chuckles and pulls me into a hug. "I couldn't hate you. Never."

"I know you might not think so, but I tried. I really did." I lean against his T-shirt. "Why didn't we work?"

Gently, he takes my shoulders and holds me back so I have to look at him. His smile is sad and maybe the tiniest bit bitter. "Maybe it's because someone else had your heart before I ever got to it."

My first instinct is to deny it, but what's the point

now? We're over. It's better just to move on.

He glances at his watch. "Didn't you have an appointment to get to? I'm afraid you're going to be late."

"I don't think I really need to go now."

"I'm still taking you to prom," Grant says. "I wouldn't ditch you like that."

I shake my head, feeling ill. I'm going to miss my senior prom. I'm going to miss the prom that I've practically designed from start to finish.

"Are you sure?" he asks, his eyes worried. "You've worked so hard on this. I don't want to be the reason you miss it."

I know what would happen if we went tonight. We'd dance under the stars, laugh at a candlelit table. It would be magical and perfect, and we'd end up right back together again, repeating the cycle that we're doomed to repeat until we finally walk away for good.

It's better now than later. It hurts, but it would hurt more down the road. Resentment will begin to grow between us, and I don't ever want to resent Grant. I want to remember these last few months as being a sweet gift. No, maybe we weren't perfect for each other, but I still dated the kindest, most popular boy in high school.

How many girls can say that?

But it's time to say goodbye.

Instead of answering him, I lean in and give him one last soft kiss. "It's just a dance, right? I'll be fine. Besides, now you don't have to wear that vest you hated."

He looks like he's going to argue, but then he just gives me a small smile. "I really do hate that vest."

I swipe at my eyes and laugh. "I know you do."

I slide into my car, feeling numb. I'm not going to prom. Grant and I just broke up.

I'm not going to prom.

A solitary tear slides down my cheek, and it's soon followed by another. I take out my phone and dial Riley's number. It immediately goes to her voice mail.

My heart aches, and I need to talk to someone. I don't want to call Mom. I can't call Dad.

There's only one option left, and I'm not excited about it.

"Lauren?" my brother says when he answers the phone. "Can't figure out the controls on the TV again?"

I lose it. I bawl into my phone, telling Brandon everything.

And my stupid, annoying, jerky older brother talks to me for thirty minutes, telling me it's going to be all right, telling me I made the right choice.

"It's awful," I say after most of the tears have

ebbed. "But the worst thing is that I'm going to miss prom. I've worked so hard, and I'm going to miss it."

"You're such a girl," Brandon says, his voice teasing. "Your boyfriend breaks up with you, and all you can think about is the dress you'll never wear."

I know he's trying to lighten the mood, but I hiccup and start to sob again.

It's a really fabulous dress.

"Listen," Brandon says. "You don't need a date. Go alone, hang out with Riley, dance with anyone you want."

"I can't just go by myself," I gasp, appalled at the very thought.

"Yes, you can. Because you're awesome, and you don't need a guy to confirm that."

I close my eyes. "Okay."

"I mean it," he says, using his stern voice. "You get yourself to that dance, do you understand?"

"Yes."

"Good. Now you better go because you only have seven hours to get beautiful, and trust me—you're going to need every minute."

He laughs at his joke, thinking he's terribly funny. I have to hold back a watery smile, amused with how pleased he is with himself.

"Thanks, Brandon."

"Anytime—as long as it's after nine in the

morning. No early morning calls, got it?"

I roll my eyes, say goodbye, and then end the phone call.

I'm going to prom. Alone. All by myself.

This is going to be the worst night.

My gown is a stunning confection of pale pink fabric. The bodice is satin, and the skirt is embellished with sparkles galore. It flares out at my hips and falls to the floor in a waterfall of chiffon.

It's everything I've dreamed of and more.

If I only had a date, it would be perfect.

As I'm brooding, I accidentally poke myself in the eye with my mascara wand. I blink several times, trying to clear my vision. When I can see again, I find a dark smudge right under my eye. Growling, I wipe it away and touch up my under-eye concealer.

Without the makeup, it would be very obvious that I've been crying most of the day. Luckily, concealer is almost as fabulous as glitter.

I ended up skipping my nail and hair appointment. I wasn't up for the stylist's inquisitive questions. She'd want to know what I was wearing, who I was going with...why I was crying.

At this point, I just want to see my decorated tables.

With my hair twisted in a simple chignon instead of in an elaborate updo, I get into my car. Mom and Dad are already gone for the weekend, so there's no one to snap pictures of me leaving.

Thank goodness.

I arrive at the botanical gardens five minutes early, but several people on the committee have already beat me. They're putting the plain white tablecloths on the tables, and I'm just in time to help with the sequined tops. The setting sun sinks low, and the garden lights flicker on in the dusky, tree-shaded light.

After the tablecloths are in place, I place the coral and pink peony centerpieces. Finally, I turn on the battery operated candles at each table.

"It looks amazing!" Janna gushes after I place the last light. "So much better than the convention center."

It does look amazing. It's just as beautiful as I had hoped it would be.

A slight breeze blows through, and it carries with it the warmth of the day. It will be a beautiful night.

But I've seen enough. It's time to go home.

"I'm leaving," I tell Janna.

She looks horrified. "You're what?"

"I'm leaving," I repeat. "I just wanted to let you know in case there was anything else you wanted me to take care of first."

"It nearly killed us to get all this together. Are you

sure you can't stay?" She motions to my dress. "At least for a little while?"

Riley is coming with a guy I don't know. She'll be busy all night, and I don't want to crash her evening. All the guys will have dates, so there will be no one to dance with.

"I'm sure."

She looks at me like I've lost my mind, but I stride from my fairyland garden anyway. Just as couples are arriving, I sweep my sparkling gown into the car, unpin my hair, and drive away from prom.

Chapter Twenty-one
May 21st - Cont.

"What do you mean you're not coming to prom!" Riley exclaims.

"I mean I'm not coming to prom."

I thought the sentiment was rather self-explanatory.

"Lauren!" Riley whines. "You have to come!"

With a long sigh, I lean my head against the back of the couch. The house is lonely with my parents gone and Harrison off in Connecticut.

Just the thought of Harrison makes my heart flutter, but just as soon as it does, a wave of guilt washes over me.

Poor Grant. He was right. My heart was always somewhere else.

"You'll have a good time," I assure Riley. "I would be such terrible company tonight. All I've done is cry."

She makes a soft, sad noise. "I'm sorry I pushed you into it, Lauren."

I close my eyes. "Pushed me into what?"

"Dating Grant. You were so hesitant; I should have known it wouldn't work."

"Why did you want us together so badly?" I ask, curious.

There's a pause. "I knew you and Harrison had a thing for each other, and I wanted him."

I don't know what to say to that.

"I'm so sorry," she says in a rush. "It was wrong, and he didn't end up liking me anyway."

Part of me wants to be upset with her, but I didn't have to start dating Grant. That was my choice. I shouldn't have gone out with him when I was so hung up on someone else.

"Are you mad?" Riley asks.

"Of course not. It doesn't matter now."

"There's still time for you to get here. You'll only be a little late."

I glance out the darkening windows. The dance only started thirty minutes ago, and I haven't changed out of my dress yet. I could go...

"No, not tonight. I'm going to watch lame television shows and cry into a tub of ice cream."

"Lauren—"

"Go dance. Stop ignoring your date."

"Are you still coming over tonight?"

"No. I'm going to sit on the couch and wallow."

She makes a disgusted noise, but she finally lets me go. When she hangs up, I'm left with a dull ache in my chest.

I'm just about to settle in for the night when my phone rings. I expect to see Riley's number again, her trying one more time to convince me to join her, but it's Mom.

"Hey," I answer. "Did you guys get to your hotel?"

"I didn't expect you to answer," she says, concern lacing her voice. "I thought I'd have to leave a message. You haven't been carrying your phone around the dance, waiting for my call, have you?"

Ugh. I have to tell her.

"I'm so sorry, Laur," she says after I finish. "But are you sure you don't want to stay with Riley tonight? I'd feel better if you weren't there all alone."

"Mom—"

"Yes, I know." She laughs, but she still sounds concerned. "You're fine by yourself for one weekend. I'd just feel better if Harrison were home."

My stomach flip-flops at his name, but I keep my thoughts silent.

"The Millers are right next door," I remind her. "And I have a car in case of emergencies. I'll be fine—really."

"Just be careful."

"I will be."

She promises to call tomorrow, and then she hangs up.

I glance around the quiet living room. The only sound is the steady thrum of the clock ticking. Slightly unnerved, I go up to my bedroom to change.

Before I take the dress off, I stop in front of the vanity to admire it. When will I have a chance to wear it again? It's now or never. Even if there is no one here to see it, it's better than not wearing it at all.

I leave the dress on but take out my earrings. The pink-stone studded chandelier earrings match the dress, but they're heavy, and now that my hair is down, strands keep twining in them. My hand slides over Harrison's jewelry box. When I lift the lid, I find the necklace that Grant gave me. It's carefully coiled into one of the earring compartments, but it's always felt out of place there.

Just like it's always felt out of place around my neck.

Exchanging the necklace for the earrings, I take the chain out and drape it over my hand. Should I give it back? Is it wrong to keep it?

No, I decide. It's mine, and the memory is a sweet one.

Still, it doesn't belong in here.

It takes me about an hour, but I've sorted through my original jewelry box. All of the necklaces are untangled, and I've even uncovered a few more pairs of earrings that were lying buried under the knotted mess of precious metal.

I carefully hang each necklace, and then I slip Grant's necklace over a hook. The citrine catches the light, sparkling subtly against the black velvet backing. Slowly, I shut the door.

It feels as if a weight has been lifted. This chapter of my life is closed, and now another is about to begin. I don't necessarily know what it holds, but I know that moving forward feels good.

Three hours later, I'm sprawled out on the couch, still in my gown. One foot is up on the armrest, the other is hanging off the edge. Penelope is curled next to my head, and every once in a while, she flicks her fluffy tail in my face.

I splutter as she does it again—this time, she aimed right for my mouth. I move my head to the side, and she stretches, thankfully moving her tail. I realize the hand I've flung over my head is starting to fall asleep. I'm just debating shifting when I hear tires crunching in the gravel in the drive.

I stiffen, nervous.

Headlights shine behind the blinds in the side window, and the vehicle travels toward the guest house. Adrenaline pumps through my body, and I pull myself off the couch. Staying away from the windows, I slink into the kitchen, trying to covertly look out the back window.

A door shuts, and I peek out.

The figure is tall with a handsome silhouette. A familiar silhouette.

Harrison looks tired, almost dejected. He fights with his keys, trying to find the one that will open the guest house.

Rushing across the room, I toss the French doors open.

He turns, startled.

He's dressed in a tux, but the tie hangs loose at his throat. His hair is softly mussed, looking as if he's been running a hand through it.

His eyes drift over me, taking in my dress and bare feet. I brush my hair behind my shoulder, self-conscious.

"I thought you'd be at the dance." His voice is soft in the night.

The patio stones are cool under my feet as I take a step forward. "I thought you were at a wedding."

Almost hesitant, he strides to me, his tuxedo jacket carelessly tossed over his arm. "I was."

"You weren't supposed to be back until tomorrow."

"I decided to come home early."

The moon shines above us, almost full, lighting the patio with its soft glow. The smell of spring is in the air, and it envelopes us.

"Why?" I ask.

A quick smile flashes across his face, and then he looks down. When he looks back up again, his expression is slightly guarded. "Brandon called me."

I cross my arms. "Oh?"

He takes a step closer. "He said you and Grant broke up. He wanted me to check on you, make sure you were all right."

A soft, warm feeling flutters in my stomach. "You took a three-hour flight to make sure I was all right?"

"No."

Startled, I swallow.

He moves closer still. "I took a three-hour flight to take you to prom."

My knees go weak, and I place a hand on a patio chair to keep my balance.

"But the flight was delayed," he continues, sounding weary. "And it took forever to get through security."

I nod, too overwhelmed to answer. My thoughts are chaotic, jumping from one place to another. My emotions are a jumbled mess.

"I knew how much the night meant to you," he says. "I didn't want you to have to go alone." He gently tugs on a strand of my hair. "You did go, didn't you?"

Looking away, I shrug.

"Not even for a little bit?"

"I finished setting up, but I left before anyone got there." I meet his eyes and sigh. "It looked amazing."

Harrison lets my hair drop. "I'm sure it did."

Unable to bear the weight of his gaze, I look at the moon.

"If you didn't go, what's with the dress?" he asks.

Ah, yes. The dress.

"I just wanted to wear it. It's not like I'll get another chance."

He nods, looks into the night, and then asks, "Where are your parents?"

"Dad's seeing the shoulder specialist in Missoula."

"Right...right. I knew that." A pause. "You're here by yourself?"

I give him a wry look. "I'm eighteen, you know. Not exactly a baby."

He studies me, but his expression is schooled, and his eyes aren't giving anything away.

I cringe at the smallest twinge of disappointment. He may have come back to take me to prom, but he still sees a high school girl when he looks at me.

"You want to come in?" I ask, turning. "I haven't eaten all the ice cream yet."

"That's a little cliche, isn't? Drowning your sorrows

in Rocky Road?"

"Mint chip," I correct as I pull the tub from the freezer. "Rocky Road is reserved for major heartbreaks."

Harrison lays his tux jacket on the back of a barstool and raises an eyebrow. "Oh yeah? And how would you class this one?"

I plop the ice cream between us and dig a spoon into the green and brown-flecked ice cream. "Class two. Maybe a two-point-five."

"Oh yeah?" He takes the spoon from me.

I shrug. "It sucks, but I'm glad I wasn't the one who had to initiate it."

Harrison pauses mid-bite. "Grant broke up...with you?"

Stealing the suspended spoonful of ice cream from him, I say, "It was sort of mutual, but it was his idea."

Penelope jumps on the counter, and I nudge her down. She hops to the barstool next to Harrison, her tail twitching in irritation until Harrison scratches behind her ear.

She settles on her haunches and begins to purr as he continues to stroke her back.

Oh, to be that cat.

"How was the wedding?" I ask, changing the subject.

He grimaces. "Fine."

I laugh at the expression on his face. "Fine?"

"My cousin isn't too happy with me."

It's getting late, and I hide a yawn behind my hand. "Did you trip on the stairs and take out the bridesmaids? Give a really awful speech at the reception?"

"Actually..." He looks away, carefully avoiding my eyes. "I skipped the reception."

"You skipped the—" I stop suddenly, the truth of it sinking in. "You skipped the reception so you could get on the plane."

He gives me a small smile. "What are friends for, right?"

Friends...

For the first time ever, I hate that word. Friends? I don't want to be friends with Harrison. I'm friends with Riley. I would even say I'm friends with Grant. But Harrison? I want to be so much more than friends. Even if it means waiting until I graduate.

Which I'm pretty sure is what it means.

He narrows his eyes, tilts his head to the side. "What's that look?"

Taking another bite of ice cream, I only smile.

I can wait. We can be *friends* for two weeks.

And then he better watch out, because, after that, he's mine.

Chapter Twenty-two
May 22nd

"So tell me the truth, are you devastated about missing prom?" Harrison says.

I give him a withering look and cross my ankles behind the barstool footrest. "Let's scrub lemon juice and salt in the wound, shall we?"

Harrison laughs and flips a grilled cheese sandwich on the griddle. The first time he set the temperature too high, and the bread cooked to a charcoaled crisp. He swears he won't burn this one, and even though it looks a little blackened on the edges, I don't comment on it.

"I'm just saying, you put all that time into it," he says. "You have to be disappointed."

Disappointed? Now that I'm over the shock of the breakup, I'm sick over prom. More than I'm upset about Grant.

And that just shows you how warped my priorities are.

"I'm fine."

He raises an eyebrow, obviously disagreeing with me.

Actually, I'm proud of myself for doing so well. After Harrison and I finished off the entire tub of ice cream last night, I went to bed. I only looked at my dress longingly for a few seconds before I hung it in the back of my closet.

I even slept fine, which I feel a little guilty about, to tell you the truth.

This breakup is going far better than it should. Poor Grant.

I slept in and then got up and ready for the day. I even did a short video for my blog before I heard Harrison rummaging around in the kitchen.

Now Harrison is making me an early lunch, working under the assumption that I'm too brokenhearted to feed myself.

"I'm only asking because I might have a job opportunity for you."

What does a job have to do with prom?

I raise an eyebrow, waiting for him to continue.

"We're having this thing for work..." He trails off, scrutinizing the sandwich, probably wondering why the bread is done but the cheese is cold.

"A 'thing?'"

Obviously deciding the sandwich is fine, he slides it onto a plate and hands it to me. "It's a party of sorts. The Harbinger Hotel is having a soiree to celebrate its imminent opening, and all the bigwigs are flying in. They've invited the entire firm. There's going to be speeches and slide shows, and the whole thing will be rather boring, to tell you the truth."

"Okay?"

Realizing he hasn't gotten to his point yet, he says, "The event coordinator met with a group of us last week to discuss the length of the speeches and so on. She mentioned her assistant went on maternity leave, and she's shorthanded."

Now my interest is peaked. "Oh, yeah?"

"I might have made a call for you this morning."

Suddenly terrified, I exclaim, "Harrison! I have absolutely no experience in event planning."

He cocks his head to the side.

"Well," I say, "not professional event planning."

"You'd be fine. It's not like you're putting together the entire thing. You'd just be helping out."

I take a bite of the sandwich and chew carefully. The buttery bread melts in my mouth, but the cheese is still solid. "I guess I could think about it..."

Harrison grins and starts another sandwich. "That's good. Because you have a meeting with her

Monday afternoon."

I give him an incredulous look.

He only laughs. "You'll love it. The event is black tie and everything…you'll be able to wear your dress."

"The help doesn't usually attend these things," I say.

"Sure they do." He sounds completely confident.

I finish off another bite. "Even if I do get to go, I'll probably have to wear black slacks and hide in the corners of the room, earpiece in my ear, waiting for party emergencies."

"I think you have event coordinator's assistant confused with a secret agent." Harrison grins to himself. "Secret agent Laura-Lou."

He starts to hum a popular spy movie theme.

"You are a pain."

He looks up, a smile on his lips, and his green-blue eyes lock with mine. "I'm a pain who cooked you lunch and got you a job.

"You don't know I'll get the job."

Harrison shakes his head. "Yes, I do. I went through your phone this morning, found Janna's number, and had her text me pictures from the dance last night. I ended up sending them to Carla, and she was very impressed."

"You did *what?*"

He only grins. "You're welcome."

Chapter Twenty-three
May 23rd

I've never been so nervous in my life. What was Harrison doing, thinking he could get me a job? I don't remember saying I wanted a job. I certainly wasn't looking for one.

Get an associate's degree, marry someone fabulous, adopt two springer spaniel puppies, and hopefully continue my craft blog—that's the plan.

The plan.

A secretary steps into the foyer of a small but immaculately decorated office. It has a modern but comfortable feel, prestigious but welcoming, and it's all done in various shades of cream and white. The only splashes of color come from the various bouquets of fresh flowers.

If I were here to book an event, I would be enchanted.

But right now, I'm just slightly nauseous.

"Carla's ready to see you now."

I stand and smooth down my knee-length brown skirt. I've paired a white sleeveless blouse and a pair of sensible, non-sparkly heels with it. Trying to look professional, I toned down the accessories.

A tall, voluptuous woman with short blond hair steps forward to greet me as soon as I'm through the door. She's wearing cropped navy slacks, a well-cut polka-dot blouse, and bright yellow, sky-high heels. She looks like she walked out of a fashion magazine.

I don't think I had to tone down my outfit.

"I'm Carla." She gives me a firm handshake. "You must be Lauren."

"That's right." I try to pretend I'm not nervous.

Carla tells me to take a seat, and then she sits at her desk. She folds her hands, her expression friendly. "As I'm sure Harrison has already told you, my assistant is out for a couple months. I'm looking for someone to fill in for her only temporarily, until early July, I believe. Normally I would be looking for someone with prior experience, but since you've worked on events at your school, I think you just might fit the bill. Tell me a little about your experience on the prom committee and any other events you've helped with."

Self-conscious at first, I go on to tell her. I grow more confident as I realize there have been several things I've been involved in, not just dances but theater events and fundraisers as well.

When I mention my blog, her eyes light with interest, and she pulls it up on her screen. "You've done all this?"

I nod, again nervous now that she's browsing my site.

"This is lovely. You're obviously very crafty." She closes her laptop. "I have to warn you, though. I mostly need someone to run errands—get me coffee. Is that all right?"

"Yes, of course."

She smiles brightly. "All right then, consider yourself hired. When do you graduate?"

"Next Tuesday."

"Good." She stands. "Perhaps you can help me in the afternoons and weekends until then, and then after that, we'll set a more solid schedule."

I thank her and walk through the office in a daze.

Chapter Twenty-four
May 28th

In the next week, I find myself calling florists, talking to contractors, and, of course, buying lots of lattes.

Today I arrive at the Harbinger, my hands full with two coffee carriers and bags of gold balloons, metallic ribbon, and stacks of various-sized silver card stock stars.

"Lauren," Carla calls from inside the ballroom. "Over here."

I try not to gawk at the huge area and tall vaulted ceilings. There's a spiral staircase in front of me, leading up to a second loft-style level. Already tables and chairs are being brought in for Harrison's firm's event on Saturday.

"It's a great space, isn't it?" Carla looks around in appreciation and then says to me, "We do a lot of events for Rogers, Fredmont, and Claude." She turns to the man next to her. "But I think this is my favorite of your buildings so far."

The man smiles, looking genuinely friendly. He extends his hand, relieving me of the coffees, which are shifting precariously in my hands. "I'm Albert Fredmont."

It's Harrison's boss. For some reason, the thought makes me horribly nervous.

"Lauren Alderman, sir."

He turns to Carla. "Your new assistant?"

"That's right. Your Harrison recommended her, in fact."

"He did, did he?" Mr. Fredmont smiles. "Well, then I'm sure she is a good choice."

I feel a flush of pride for Harrison.

"He was here, somewhere, but I think he went back to the office." Mr. Fredmont pauses. "Lauren, you said, right?"

I freeze. "Yes, sir."

"Lauren who's graduating Tuesday?"

Gulping, I nod.

"He asked for the day off to go to your graduation. Congratulations."

"Oh, thank you."

I didn't know Harrison was going to take off for the ceremony. A blush rises to my cheeks, and I try not to smile like an idiot.

Mr. Fredmont discusses a few more things with Carla, and then he excuses himself.

"Set the stars over on that table," Carla says. "And any other supplies I have you bring. We'll begin set up on Friday morning. You called the florist?"

"Yes, the bouquets will be ready to pick up at eleven."

"I'll leave you in charge of those. You can take the van." Carla looks at her clipboard. "Did you call the caterer?"

I nod. "They are completely peanut free, and the vegetarian dishes are prepared in coconut oil, not lard or any other kind of animal fat."

"Thank you for thinking to check on that."

She sets her clipboard aside and takes a sip of her latte. She closes her eyes in appreciation. "That other one is for you," she says, motioning to the last drink.

The others were swooped up almost as soon as Mr. Fredmont set them down.

"Oh, I don't..." I force myself to smile and pick up the cardboard cup. "Thank you."

She wraps me in a one-armed hug. "It's the least I can do when I plan to work you to death the same week you graduate."

Then she spots one of the hotel staff attempting to move one of her tables, and she's off, clicking across the marble floor in her less than sensible heels.

Laughing, I take a tentative sip of my drink. It's sweet—very sweet. And there's coffee in there, I'm pretty sure, but it's fairly well covered up by the sugar.

Truthfully, it's not bad. I take another tiny taste.

"Looks like they're making a grown-up out of you," a voice whispers in my ear.

I pause mid-sip. Just hearing Harrison's voice makes me fluttery. I turn slowly, trying to school my expression so I don't look like a starstruck architect groupie...if there is such a thing.

Harrison's dressed for work in a suit. He's pressed and perfect, and I want to loosen his tie, mess up his hair.

Without asking permission, he takes a sip of my coffee. "Wow, that's...sugary."

"It hides the coffee flavor."

He gives me a lopsided smile that lights his eyes. "I see."

"I met Mr. Fredmont," I say. "You seem to have pulled the wool over his eyes."

Handing my coffee back, Harrison says, "Why's that?"

I shrug. "He actually likes you, so he obviously doesn't know you that well."

Harrison leans against the wall. "You know me very well, and you like me."

"Like you? I do not." I raise my eyebrows, a smile

on my lips.

"Liar." He whispers the word, and a thrill runs through me, straight to my toes.

I bite the inside of my cheek so I won't grin at him. "I have to get back to work."

"Run off Laura-Lou." He raises his eyebrows slowly. "I'll see you at home."

There's something so domestic about it, so insanely delicious, that this time, I can't hold back my grin.

Chapter Twenty-five
May 31st

Brandon sticks his head in my room. "Mom says we need to leave in five minutes."

I adjust my graduation cap, trying to get it to sit right. No matter what I do with my hair, it looks awful.

"All right." I sigh.

It's as good as it's going to get.

My parents and Harrison wait for me in the kitchen.

"I look ridiculous," I say as I enter the room.

"You do not look ridiculous." Mom steps forward to fuss with my cap. When she steps back, she blinks a few times, overcome. "You're all grown up."

If Grant were here, I'd be mortified, but for some reason, it doesn't bother me to have Harrison see my parents all weepy and sentimental. Like Dad said when he moved in, he practically grew up here. My family

257

is as much his as they are mine.

The thought makes me warm, and I have to look away.

"You ready to graduate?" Dad asks.

I nod, suddenly nervous. Everything's different after this. There are no more classes, no more dances or plays.

We arrive at the stadium with seven minutes to spare. Riley's already here, and she bounces over when she sees me.

"We're graduating!" With one hand on her cap, she twirls.

I laugh at her. "You say it like you were worried."

In all the years we've known each other, neither of us has ever failed a class, never even gotten close.

"Of course not." She sets her hands on her hips, cheer-style. "But it's still a big deal, don't you think?"

Big deal? It's monumental. After today, I'll no longer be a high school student. The moment I accept my diploma, that wall keeping Harrison and me apart is going to crumble.

After today, he's fair game.

As I look at my classmates hugging and high-fiving, I chew my lip. Harrison hasn't mentioned it, though. He hasn't even hinted that things will change between us. He still flirts and teases, but he always did that.

"Hey, Lauren," Grant says from behind me.

We haven't talked much since we broke up, nothing more than a quick exchange of friendly greetings in the halls.

"Hi, Grant."

There's a dull ache in my heart, even a bit of regret, but mostly I'm just happy he's still speaking with me—happy that he doesn't hate me.

"Congratulations." He stands, stiff and awkward, and then his expression softens, and he pulls me in a hug. "You look beautiful."

I hug him back. "You too. But, you know, handsome."

He pulls back and smiles. "Are you still sticking around here after graduation?"

I nod. "I'm going to go to the university. What about you? Still heading to Missoula?"

"Yeah."

Just another reason we wouldn't have worked.

Grant's eyes are a little sad. "Goodbye, Lauren."

"Goodbye, Grant."

"It's time!" Riley grabs my arm and drags me to the front of the line, thinking that if she doesn't deposit me, I'll somehow wander off, lost.

I'm second in line, right after Kevin Aarons. Riley sifts through the others to find her place in the middle.

With Kevin in front of me, we step into the

stadium. The sun is hot today, and the smell of freshly-cut grass is in the air. Families and friends sit in the bleachers, watching us trail like ants to our seats.

The folding chair is hot. For the first time today, I'm glad for the graduation gown and the extra layer of protection from the scorching metal.

We finally begin, and about fifteen minutes into the speeches, my attention wanders. I remember sitting in the stadium several years ago, watching Brandon in this same chair. He was second in line, too.

The following summer was the same, but in the autumn, he left for college. I went from being a baby sister to an only child.

I wonder how different my life will be next fall.

After what seems like forever with the late May sunshine beating down on us, we begin our walk to the front.

"Lauren Alderman," the principal announces.

I accept my diploma, smile for the camera, and march through the middle of the aisle to meager applause. It seems to take forever for the rest of my class to accept their diplomas. Riley walks up the constructed stage, proud and pretty in her cap and gown, and the crowd goes wild when she accepts it. I cheer right along with them.

Finally, the ceremony is finished. The principal announces us, the graduating class, and we toss our caps into the air.

And then it's over.

I'm an adult.

I pick my way through a crowd of my exuberant classmates. My heels make it tricky to navigate in the grass, and I'm watching my footing more than I'm watching my back. Suddenly I'm grabbed around the middle and lifted into the air.

"Brandon!" I squeal. "Put me down!"

My brother laughs and deposits me back on the ground. Just as soon as my feet touch, I'm assaulted again, this time by Riley. She hugs me tight, laughing.

Then she bursts into tears.

"Riley!" I teeter, trying to keep my balance. "Why are you crying?"

"Because it's over," she sniffs. "I won't see you every day! We won't have classes together."

I laugh and pat her back. "Of course we'll still see each other. It's not like we're going to different colleges."

She lets me go and dabs her eyes with her finger, trying to be careful not to smear her eye makeup. "It's not the same."

Once Riley finally composes herself, Mom steps over and hugs me. She, too, starts to get a little weepy, and I soothe her as well. Dad waits his turn, and thank goodness he's composed, or I might start to get misty myself.

Then there's Harrison. He stands, his hands in his pockets, his eyes on me. The world fades; he's all I see. All I want to see.

He steps forward and opens his arms to me. I step into them, and time stands still. He smells as he always does, of light aftershave and deodorant and guy. I breathe him in, wishing I could stay here for the rest of the day.

Too soon, he releases me and steps back.

I watch him, waiting for some sign that things will be different between us now. Hoping something has changed. But there's nothing in his gaze that wasn't there this morning. No hint, no promise.

Somewhat disappointed, I let out a subtle exhale and turn back to my family.

"We're going to lunch," Mom announces. "I'm starving. Riley, go ask your family to join us."

Obedient, she runs off. Soon she, her parents, and her seven-year-old twin brothers join us. Brandon asks where Harper is, but Riley informs him she's off talking. He looks disappointed and scans the crowd, looking for her. After a little discussion, we decide on a chain restaurant outside the mall.

As soon as we reach the car, I take off my graduation gown. The cheap material was hot and it itched, and I'm happy to be free of it. After tossing it in the back, I slip into my seat. Brandon and Harrison are riding in the back, so we're not all squished in here like we were the night Riley joined us for dinner.

I steal a peek at Harrison, but he's talking to Brandon, not paying me any attention.

The minute we get to the restaurant, Brandon turns to goo when he sees Harper stepping out of Riley's car. He strides to her, trying to act cool, but it's so apparent he's in love with her.

Riley steps next to me and stares at the pair, doe-eyed. Then her brothers squeal, and one darts away from the car. Riley runs into the parking lot, grabbing him just before their mother reaches him.

"We need to talk," Harrison says from my shoulder. His voice is quiet, insistent.

A riot of butterflies explodes in my belly, making me feel light and giddy.

"We do?" I ask, nonchalant.

Neither of us looks at each other. We're just standing side by side, waiting to go in the restaurant.

"We do. After lunch?"

I shiver, excitement building in my muscles. After lunch?

After lunch?

How am I supposed to wait that long?

"That's fine," I answer.

Finally, our group is intact and we head inside.

The air is thick with the smell of hamburgers, pizza, and French fries. My stomach growls in anticipation.

Somehow I make it through the entire meal with a calm and collected appearance. On the inside, I'm a chaotic flurry of nerves.

We split up with Riley's family after the meal is over, and both her mom and mine coo over the two of us, telling us how proud they are.

Finally, we're back home. I slide out of the car, unsure where to stand. Should I go in? Should I wait for him here?

The decision is made for me when he joins my side. Brandon and my parents head to the house, but we hang behind.

I cross my arms, not wanting him to see how exhilarated I am.

"Are you going to be working the party on Saturday?" he asks.

My spirits fall only a little. "No, Carla said only she needs to be there. I think she was doing me a favor not making me work it."

He crosses his arms, mimicking me. "I have an extra ticket. You can come if you want. Technically, it's a plus-one on my ticket, but it doesn't have to be a date."

Is he saying that he doesn't want it to be a date? Or that it's not a date unless I want it to be?

I hesitate. This conversation isn't going at all the way I'd hoped.

"I'd like to see it," I finally answer. "So, thank you."

A smile shines in his eyes. "You'll come?"

I nod, feeling the butterflies take flight again. "Yes, I'll come."

Chapter Twenty-Six
June 4th

On the morning of the big night, I'm put in charge of filling the balloons with helium from the huge tank. After I knot the ends, I attach a long piece of ribbon and tie a star at the bottom. When I release them, the balloons bob to the ceiling, and the metallic stars hang from their long tails.

I've already done hundreds of them. They're the coolest thing I've ever seen.

"How's it going, Lauren?" Carla asks as she wanders over.

She and her clipboard have been everywhere this morning, supervising. The hotel staff doesn't seem to like her very much, but the ballroom has been transformed.

The tables are set with crisp red linens, and on them sit real white porcelain plates and gleaming silverware. The centerpieces are simple white roses arranged in small silver bowls.

Besides the stars, there are subtle metallic accents everywhere—the threads stitched into the napkins, the platters that are ready for the dessert table.

"I'm almost done here." I fill up another balloon and then nod to the center of the room. "And then I'll hunt down someone to remove that ladder. It's been bugging me all morning."

"Good girl." Carla puts her checklist down. "You checked that the deliveries were signed for?"

"Yes, everything is here."

She nods, writing things down, and then pauses before she walks away. "You're going to the local university, right?"

As I tie on a string, I nod.

"What are you going to be studying?"

The knot keeps slipping from my fingers, and I scowl at it. "I'm not sure yet."

"You're good at this," Carla says. "And it seems like you enjoy it. Have you thought of being an event coordinator?"

I never had before, but in the last few weeks, it's certainly been on my mind.

"How about you look into getting a business degree to begin with, and if you're interested, we might just keep you on even after Natalia gets back from maternity leave."

The knot finally tightens over the balloon, and I look up. "Really?"

"Yes. If you want it, you have a position."

And just like that, I have a permanent job.

"Thank you!"

My boss gives me a warm smile, and then she's off to another task.

"Carla?"

She glances back.

"If I'm invited to one of our events as a guest, it's all right to go, isn't it?"

Her face is open in pleasant surprise. "Who are you going with?"

"Harrison," I say, and my ears feel hot.

"Of course it's all right. Have a good time." Carla smiles and tilts her head. "And if there's some emergency, it's good to know I'll have an extra hand."

Her words sound ominous, but I'm glad to hear her say there are event emergencies.

I knew there were.

I'll be sure to inform Harrison.

The day goes by in a blur of one task followed by another. There are people everywhere: hotel staff, our team, uppity hotel types, and even one of the partners from Harrison's firm I haven't met yet. A band has been brought in for the event, and they're setting up next to the piano, doing sound checks and scurrying about, looking for extension cords.

It's nearing late afternoon, and we're just wrapping up here. My hair appointment is in thirty minutes. I'm cutting it close, but the salon isn't far from here.

I'm finishing the final touches on the place cards, making sure I have everyone in the correct spot. I pause when the next card up is Harrison's. There, next to him, is me.

I give a girlish squeal as I place my card.

I've just finished with the last table when I hear someone yell for Carla that the ice sculptures have arrived.

The large double doors at the back are opened, and all at once, a great gust of wind blows through the room. The balloons and stars shimmy in the breeze, but the hundreds of place cards I've just placed are picked up and scattered about the room.

I gasp, "No!"

But there's nothing I can do but watch them fly to the floor.

Scrunching my brow, I place a hand on my forehead. Apparently I'm not meant to make a hair appointment.

One by one, I begin to pick up the cards, sorting them into alphabetical order as I go. Carla hollers at someone to hurry with the sculptures and shut the door, but I block the noise out, focusing on my task alone.

An hour and twenty minutes later, the cards have been sorted, the seating chart consulted, and everything is, once again, in its place.

"Good, Lauren," Carla says when I tell her I've finished. "Off with you now, go get beautiful for tonight."

I hurry home, only yelling a hello to my family as I rush up the stairs. I don't even bother to wait until the shower warms; I step right in, shivering in the cold water as I shampoo my hair.

After I'm properly shaved, scrubbed, and rinsed, I snap off the shower, wrap a towel around myself, and dart to my room. My dress is waiting in my closet, but I pause when I spot a small white box on my bed. Curious, I glance around my room as if I will find the answer to who left it there.

Gingerly, I open the lid. Then I let out a disappointed breath. There's only a note.

Second row, third drawer, fifth spot.

I bite my lip, grinning. When I open the correct drawer of the jewelry box Harrison gave me, I find another note.

Top lid, right-side compartment.

"Honestly, Harrison," I say under my breath. "And you all say I'm dramatic."

When I open the lid, I find them, right under the glittery heart. A pair of perfect pink, sparkling stud earrings sits against the velvet, winking up at me.

I glance at the box in my hand. Printed in tiny gold writing on the inside lid, it reads, twenty-four karat gold, genuine pink sapphires.

Next to them is, of course, another note.

A little sparkle to celebrate a successful first event.

And my heart seizes. If this is just an amicable gesture, if this is just a night out as friends, I'll die a little.

Surely not, though. This electricity, this spark, can't be one-sided.

I slip the earrings in and admire them in my vanity mirror. My dripping wet hair and towel take away from the look, but the earrings themselves are lovely.

Then, having taken too much time cooing over the gift, I rush to finish getting ready. I exchange my towel for a robe and then do my makeup and hair.

Worried I look too young, I pin my hair up in a careful updo. I would have much rather had someone else do it for me, but I make do with something simple. I'm just slipping on my dress when I hear the back door open downstairs. Harrison's muffled voice joins my mother's.

Taking a deep breath, I assess my reflection in the

mirror. I look good. Very good.

I hope Harrison thinks so.

Nervous, I go downstairs. Harrison's eyes instantly flick to me when I walk into the kitchen, and a warm sensation builds in my stomach.

His tux fits him perfectly, and he looks like he's just had a haircut today. He watches me, his gaze intense, and I go weak all over. I'm not even sure how I make it to him.

"Are you ready?" he asks.

"Lauren, you look lovely! You'll have to sneak in some pictures," Mom says. "I want to see everything."

My parents seem to be under the impression that this is nothing more than a business dinner of sorts. Like Harrison and I are going together simply because it pertains to our work.

I truly hope that's not what this is.

After saying goodbye to my mother, Harrison and I slip out of the door. Harrison stays quiet, and his silence is making the tension all that much worse. What is he thinking?

We're finally in the truck and headed to the hotel.

Keeping my tone light, I say, "Thank you for the scavenger hunt."

He flashes me a quick smile. "I see you found the earrings."

I examine my nails. "I love them. Truly, thank

you."

"You're welcome."

We reach the event, and a valet parks Harrison's truck. It's certainly a little different than parking out back and taking the three-minute walk like I've been doing all week.

Even though I know what to expect, I gasp when we cross into the ballroom. The lights have been dimmed for the party, and the floating silver stars reflect the light. There are already hundreds of guests present, and they're all in tuxes and gowns, just like in the movies.

"So this is your world, is it?" I whisper to Harrison as he leads me in.

"Apparently." He looks a little nervous. "I suppose it's yours now too."

I shake my head. "No, I wouldn't have gotten to attend tonight if you hadn't asked me."

His mouth tips in a smile. "I know."

My heart thumps, and I swallow.

A piano, violin, and cello trio play on the stage, and the soft music mingles with the quiet voices. An occasional laugh rises above the noise.

Pride in my work, in Carla's work, makes me feel all warm and fuzzy. These people are enjoying themselves, and it's because we tried so hard to make everything perfect.

"I think dinner is about to begin," Harrison says. "Let's find our seats."

"I know where they are," I whisper conspiratorially.

"Apparently, I brought the right girl."

I glance up at Harrison, ready to say something flippant, but I pause. His eyes are on mine, and his hand slides to my waist. Without a word, he draws me closer.

My heart begins to gallop, racing at a frantic rhythm that makes it impossible to catch my breath or think.

"Lauren," he says, leaning in.

Just as I'm moving to meet him, a shriek from a microphone echoes through the room. Instantly, I look away, breathing slowly to try to get a handle on my emotions.

"Sorry about that." Mr. Fredmont laughs. "Apparently, I'd never cut it as an entertainer."

The crowd laughs politely.

"Thank you all for coming this evening, and a big thanks to The Harbinger Hotel for allowing our firm to be part of their project. This hotel has been a pleasure to work on, and we are very proud of the finished product."

The crowd claps, and Harrison and I join them.

"Dinner will be served shortly. So if you can all find your seats, we'll get started."

Harrison's hand slides to my back, and he escorts me through the crowds. I hadn't noticed when I placed the cards, but we're seated with Perry Rogers, the man who started the firm.

"Harrison, who is this?" The older man stands.

"Perry, this is Lauren." Harrison nods to me. "Lauren, this is Perry, and his wife, Phyllis. Perry is my boss," he adds.

"For now," Perry says, chortling. "You'll be running the place in no time."

Harrison laughs, but he looks nervous. We sit, and I reach for his hand under the table. When I brush his palm, he winds his fingers through mine.

His hand is warm, comfortable. It makes me tingly, and I have to work to keep from grinning.

The food is served, and Perry asks the waitress for another scotch. Next to him, Phyllis, his wife, scrutinizes her plate. She holds up her hand to get the waitress's attention before she leaves.

"Yes, ma'am?" the girl asks.

Phyllis waves over her meal. "I ordered the vegetarian plate. There's some kind of sauce over the vegetables. It's not butter based, is it?"

The waitress's eyes widen. "I don't know...I'll have to check."

"It's coconut oil," I say, hoping it's all right that I'm stepping in.

Phyllis looks at me, surprised and a little skeptical that I would know.

"I've been assisting Carla in her usual assistant's absence," I explain. "I called the caterer myself. He assured me it would be cooked in coconut oil."

Perry's eyebrows rise, and he finishes off his first glass of scotch. "Well, Harrison, it looks like your girl is as efficient as you are."

I blush, wondering if Harrison will correct the man, tell him I'm not "his girl." He only squeezes my hand.

Perry speaks to Harrison through most of the meal, the conversation shifting from sports to work and then to golf. The man's already on his third scotch, and the speeches haven't even begun.

According to Carla's schedule, dancing is to follow dinner. I watch, impatient, as the band gathers on the stage. They talk for what seems like forever, and then a woman dressed in a long, slinky gown steps up to the microphone. They begin their set, doing covers of old jazz songs. People filter away from tables, and the waitstaff begins to whisk away the dishes and offer those remaining in their seats coffee.

It's all going exactly as planned.

Harrison offers me his hand. "Care to dance?"

We rise, and I murmur, "I have no idea what I'm supposed to do."

"Me either," he whispers near my ear. "Let's just swing back and forth and hope no one notices."

I laugh, and, together, we do just that.

"It's not prom," he says, and then he lowers his voice. "And there's a ridiculous amount of stuffy, pompous people here, but are you enjoying yourself?"

"I am. So much. Thank you for bringing me."

His lips tip in a warm smile, and he nudges me closer. We sway back and forth, and I rest my head against his shoulder, savoring the moment.

After several moments, Harrison clears his throat. "Lauren, I—"

"Sorry, Harrison," a man not too much older than Harrison interrupts. "Fredmont wants to introduce you to a prospective client."

Harrison turns back to me, giving me an apologetic look.

"Well, go on," I say, smiling.

Looking unsure about leaving me, Harrison nods and tells me he'll be right back. Since I don't want to go to our table by myself, I loiter toward the edges of the room, waiting for Harrison to return.

I'm relieved when I see him heading toward me, but, again, he's stopped. This time, it looks like the couple just wants to chat. He glances at me and flashes a subtly flustered look. Finally, he breaks free.

"Sorry," he says, immediately drawing me close.

"You're popular," I tease.

"Well, I'm yours now."

I stumble, and he laughs under his breath. "Falling for me, are you?"

His tone is light, but there's something there. I meet his eyes.

He lowers his voice. "There's something I wanted to talk to you—"

"Lauren!" Carla says from behind me. "I'm so glad I found you."

From Harrison's arms, I blink at my boss, startled. She looks harried, to say the least.

"There's been a glitch with the desserts."

"A glitch?" I ask.

Carla's finger taps her phone. "They're still at the bakery."

"No." I shake my head. "It was on my list. I checked on it myself—the delivery was signed for."

"Apparently it was the wrong delivery. It was cooking staples for the hotel's cafe. The woman from the bakery has left me three frantic messages, and somehow I didn't get them. Her van broke down on the way. She and several family members were able to transport the desserts back to the bakery, but she didn't have a way to bring them to us."

"Why didn't they bring them here instead of the bakery?" I rub my temples.

"She was only a few minutes away from her shop, and she was worried the frostings and things would melt without refrigeration."

"Fine," I say. "What do we do?"

Carla flashes Harrison an apologetic look. "I need you to take one of our vans and go pick them up. The woman is there, waiting for you. She'll help you get things loaded. We need them ASAP."

I glance down at my dress then close my eyes, thinking.

"Desserts are after speeches, right?" I open my eyes and nod, determined. "I can make it."

"Thank you, Lauren. I'm so sorry."

She scurries off, dialing her phone.

"We'll go together," Harrison says.

"You can't leave..."

He gives me a smile. "Of course I can."

"Are you sure?"

He nods.

Unfortunately, as we're on our way out, Mr. Fredmont corners Harrison.

"I wanted to talk to you about the Peterson project while you have a moment."

Harrison's boss drones on and on, and I simply don't have time. Harrison catches my eye, grimaces, and then nods me off.

I'm out the door, practically running through

the hotel after I leave the ballroom. My gown floats behind me, and fleetingly, I wonder if I look a bit like Cinderella fleeing from the ball.

I should have worn blue.

I get in the van, fumble with my dress, and I'm on my way to the bakery.

Luckily, there is little traffic this time of night, and I pull up in front of the building only ten minutes later. Just as Carla promised, the owner is there, waiting for me.

"I'm so sorry!" she exclaims. "I tried to get a hold of Carla."

"It's all right," I assure her. "No harm done."

She and her husband load the confections into the back. All of them are boxed, but she still warns me to drive carefully.

The thought of being responsible for it all makes me nervous, but I only nod and assure them I can handle it.

On the way back, I hit every single red light.

Every single one.

My nerves are sparking. I just know I won't make it back in time.

It takes almost ten minutes longer to reach the hotel than it did to get to the bakery, but Carla and an assortment of burly kitchen types are waiting for me.

"Hurry!" Carla grabs one of the smaller boxes and

shoves it in my hands. "Wait, I can stack one on top."

I can barely see over the layers of flat boxes.

After all this, there better be chocolate in one of these.

I follow the others into the kitchen. The waitstaff is already pulling cakes and other confections from boxes and loading serving carts.

The speeches are already going. I can hear Mr. Fredmont right now.

Carla watches as the desserts are wheeled into the ballroom, and then she sighs. "Thank you, Lauren. You're a life saver."

"I'm sorry I checked it off. It said they signed for the desserts…"

She holds up a hand, cutting me off. "This wasn't your fault. I asked you to see if they signed for it, not make sure it was in the refrigerator."

"I still feel awful."

"Don't. Now get back out there. Harrison has been pacing like a tiger since you left."

I bite my lip at the thought and hurry to the ballroom. People are again seated at their tables, but Harrison's spot is empty. Just as I start to look for him, he appears at my side.

"You made it." He grins and waves to the dessert tables, which are now being loaded up. "Good job."

"I'm sorry."

He nudges me into a private corner.

"Shouldn't you be listening?" I motion toward the man giving the current speech.

"Nah," he says, "It's all the same. A bunch of men congratulating themselves on a job well done."

I grin, and then, taking courage, I run my hand over his chest.

He steps closer and sets his hands on my shoulders. "Now, as I was saying before I was interrupted—"

"Harrison?" Someone says over the microphone. "Where has he gotten off to?"

Harrison's eyes widen with shock as he turns toward the crowd. He calls out, looking mortified but trying very hard to hide it.

"Scouting out the dessert table, were you?" The man laughs. "Get yourself up here."

"Are you supposed to do a speech?" I whisper.

"Not that I was aware of," he whispers back.

Harrison jogs forward, a picture of athletic grace in his tux.

"For those of you who haven't had the pleasure of meeting this young man yet, this is Harrison Neeley, the newest addition to our team."

I realize that the man speaking must be George Claude, the final partner in the architectural firm.

"At the early age of sixteen, Harrison began attending the University of Connecticut. He graduated with a bachelor's degree in architecture and won the nationwide contest we and Harbinger ran to design this very hotel. We are pleased he has joined our team, even if we're all a little worried he's going to be running the firm by the time he finishes with his master's. Let's give the young man a round of applause."

The room is filled with laughter and cheers, but all I can do is stare at Harrison, stunned.

I knew he was gifted, and I knew he'd won some award, but I had no idea he designed the hotel. No wonder Riley was tripping all over herself to get to him.

"Would you like to say a few words, Harrison?" George asks him.

"I...uh..." Harrison looks dumbfounded at the attention. "Actually, yes. Thank you, all. I'm honored that you gave me this opportunity...and I have no immediate plans for a hostile takeover."

The crowd laughs.

"And I'd like to do a quick shout out to the event coordinator and her staff who put all this together tonight." He motions to my boss. "Carla, it's spectacular."

She blushes and waves to the crowd.

"And can I draw your attention to the lovely girl in the pink dress standing there in the back by the desserts? That's right, turn around."

I freeze, terrified. What's he doing?

"She saved the desserts."

There are a few friendly whistles, and my face flames. I'm so glad it's dim in here.

"I'm not much of a public speaker, so I'll wrap this up," Harrison continues. "Thanks again."

Harrison steps down the stairs to a chorus of polite clapping. As he makes his way back to me, the final speaker takes the microphone.

The guests begin to wander to the dessert table. The night is dying down, and the band has already taken their leave. I wait for Harrison to bring up whatever it was he was going to tell me before we were interrupted, but there's always someone here, wanting to talk to him, wanting to congratulate him.

I help myself to a piece of chocolate ganache-covered cake and try to quell my disappointment.

"I'm sorry we didn't get to finish our dance," Harrison says from my elbow.

I wave my fork at him. "What are you talking about? I only came for the chocolate."

He smiles, knowing I'm lying.

Soon, the guests begin to filter out of the ballroom. Some linger in clusters, and Harrison is stopped several times on our way out.

Finally, we step into the warm evening. I pause, breathing in the fragrance of the night-blooming flowers in the landscaping.

"Thank you for bringing me," I say as we wait for the valet to retrieve the truck.

Harrison's hands are at his sides, and he fidgets like he's nervous. Why doesn't he just take my hand?

"You're welcome," he says. "It's a good thing you were here."

I nod, suddenly self-conscious. I thought this night would end differently.

Thirty minutes later, we pull in front of the guest house. Disappointment in the evening sits heavy in my stomach. Like a gentleman, Harrison opens my door.

We linger by the truck.

"Well...goodnight," I say, stalling.

"Thanks for coming with me."

I clasp my hands behind me. "Of course."

Why isn't he kissing me and declaring his undying affection?

Why?

"Okay." Harrison steps toward the guest house. "See you tomorrow."

I turn away, dejected.

"How was it, honey?" Mom asks when I walk in the door.

"Good." I pour a glass of water.

Mom doesn't seem to notice my listlessness as she takes an apple pie out of the oven. "Do you want some when this cools?"

"No, thanks." I drain the water. "I think I'm just going to head to bed."

In my bedroom, I stare at my dress in the reflection one last time. With a sigh, I undo the zipper and let it crumple to the floor.

I should hang it.

Instead, I step over the heap of pink chiffon and shuffle through my drawer for my most comfortable pajamas. After I've changed, I flop onto my bed and stare at the ceiling.

What was Harrison going to say? Why did he never say it?

My phone chimes, bringing me out of my melancholy brooding. I scoot down the bed to see who texted.

Come to the guest house.

I chew my lip.

Can't, I'm already in pajamas, I reply.

I don't care. Come anyway.

After several moments, I finally tell him I'll be there in a minute. I slip flip-flops on and make my way down the stairs.

Mom and Dad are watching a movie in the living room, and they don't pay me any attention as I pass through. I pause when I get to the guest house.

Should I knock? Just go in?

Feeling foolish, I rap on the door and wait for Harrison to answer.

The door slides open, and his eyes wander over me in amusement. "You really are in pajamas."

"Well...yeah." My stomach flutters when I see he's still in his tux.

"That's all right."

He pulls me inside, and I freeze.

The lights are off, but he's lit dozens of tiny tea light candles. There seems to be one everywhere there's a flat surface.

Music plays in the background, an old song I only recognize from romantic movies.

"I'm not quite as good at the decorating thing as you." He takes my hand and pulls me toward him. "But we never finished our dance, and I didn't want our night to end like that."

My chest tightens. I'm tingling all over, and my mood is bordering on euphoric.

But this is *wrong*. I look down at my pajamas, horrified.

Harrison reads the expression and laughs. "I don't care what you're wearing."

Trapping a giggle in my throat, I step into him. Just like earlier, we sway to the music.

"You know what was excruciating?" he says quietly.

"Hmmm?"

I can't believe I'm dancing with Harrison in my pajamas.

"Spending the majority of the last year watching Grant hang all over you."

Looking up, I say, "Oh?"

"I don't want to go through that again."

Harrison's warm and comfortable, and everything about him feels like home.

"What are you saying?" The words come out all breathy and embarrassing, but I barely notice.

His lips tip in his lop-sided smirk. "I'm saying you don't have to hide it anymore. We both know you're still in love with me, and I'm giving you permission to stop fighting it."

I gape at him, my temperature rising even as butterflies explode in my stomach. "Excuse me?"

Harrison pulls me closer, grinning now. "And it's possible—maybe—that I'm a little in love with you."

"Just a little?" My mouth tips in a foolish smile.

He shrugs, his fingers playing in the hair at the nape of my neck. "Maybe."

"You should stop talking," I tease.

Harrison laughs, and the sound makes me tingly. "We don't have to talk."

My knees go weak the moment he brushes his lips over mine. Standing on tip-toe, I pull him closer, sinking into him, reveling in the sensation. The spark travels all the way to my toes.

"Harrison?" I ask as he deepens the kiss.

His cheeks brush against mine as he smiles. "Hmmm?"

"How do you feel about springer spaniels?"

Startled, he pulls back and gives me the oddest look.

"Never mind." I laugh and draw him back. "There's plenty of time to talk about all that later."

Epilogue
Four Years Later

"We're not going to paint the table." Harrison crosses his arms and narrows his eyes, trying to be stern.

"Just the top? A nice cherry red, maybe?" I tease.

Of course I'm not really going to paint the table he's getting ready to stain, but he still doesn't trust me after I glittered his lamp.

He shakes his head and goes back to sanding.

We're in Harrison's new garage, which is attached to his new house, which just happens to be in the same subdivision my parents and I live in. Two houses down, in fact. The lot is huge, and even though he doesn't have a guest house, there's something better...a pool. I know where Riley and I will be all summer.

I sit on a stool, still in the dress I wore under my cap and gown from my graduation this morning. I now hold a bachelor's degree in hospitality, and I'm working full time with Carla. She's even given me a few events of my own.

Harrison finished his master's, and, genius that he is, he's now working his way to partner. Which, according to Mr. Fredmont, probably won't take that long.

I still do my craft blog, but now it's centered on events, as that's what my life revolves around these days.

"What about a little glitter?" I give him a smile. "You could sprinkle a light dusting over the stain."

He pauses, and there's something slightly mischievous in his expression, like he's been waiting for me to bring it up. "The chemical makeup of the glitter would react badly to the stain."

"What?" I laugh, protesting. "I've never heard of such a thing."

"It's true. It'll say it right on the bottle." He motions to a shelf where I left some of my craft stuff the day before. "Check for yourself."

A jar of hot pink glitter sits with the paints.

I scrunch my nose, thinking. "Did I bring that over?"

"You must have," Harrison continues sanding. "What would I be doing with it?"

What indeed?

I pick up the bottle and look it over. There is

absolutely nothing that says anything about adverse reactions to the chemicals in stains.

"Nope," I say.

"Hand it here," he says. "You must have missed it."

He stands as he takes the bottle and unscrews the top.

I set my hands on my hips and grin at him. "What? Are you going to tell me the warning is *inside* the bottle?"

"No." He laughs. "But it sounded like there was something clinking around in there. What is that?"

He peers in the jar, and then he hands it to me.

Looking at him like he's lost his mind, I poke around the glitter with my finger. "No...nothing here."

Then I freeze.

Harrison sinks to his knee in front of me, and I suck in a breath.

It's a ring—a diamond ring in the bottle of glitter.

"Lauren Louise Alderman, will you marry me?"

I'm so flustered, I end up dropping the bottle.

Glitter goes everywhere. It's on the floor...on the table he was sanding...on us.

Actually, it's mostly on him.

Harrison cringes, groaning as he tries not to laugh.

"I'm sorry!"

"It's all right," he says, still on his knee. "Do you

think you could give me an answer, though?"

Realizing I'm still standing here, I throw myself at him. "Yes! Of course, yes."

We tumble to the ground. Harrison slides the ring on my finger, and then he kisses me, ignoring the fact that we're on the garage floor and completely covered in sparkles.

I pull back slightly. "If the table is going to be half mine, that probably means we should paint half of it."

"It's already covered in glitter." Harrison gives me a look. "What more do you want?"

Nothing.

There is absolutely nothing I want more than Harrison's ring on my finger and the two of us covered in glitter.

Shine & Shimmer
Glitter & Sparkle, Book 2

Available Now

Chapter One

"I'm thinking navy with yellow and hot pink accents," I say in lieu of a hello.

Lauren, my best friend for the last ten years, doesn't miss a beat. "Awesome colors. For what?"

I adjust the cell phone at my ear and peer at the guy across the park, the one under the black fabric canopy. "My wedding."

"I'm sorry," Lauren says, "but I think you might have forgotten to mention you have a boyfriend, much less a fiance."

"I thought I should tell him first."

The day is the epitome of the perfect Montana summer Saturday. A few wispy clouds roll over a bright blue sky, and the mountain air is warm without being sweltering. It's my first summer spent apart from Lauren, but she and her new boyfriend, Harrison, are too mushy to be around right now, so I feel this will be good for our relationship. She can be starry-eyed, and I don't have to pretend I'm not green with envy.

Not that I'm jealous that she has Harrison—scrumptious as he is. It's that I want what they found. I want over the top, "no you hang up first," new love. Or a slightly less gooey, possibly more romance novel, version of it.

And luck is with me because less than twenty-four hours after arriving in my aunt's hometown, I've found my Mr. Right. He's an artist—an actual, honest-to-goodness artist.

His thick brown hair is on the long side, much longer than the jocks I typically date keep theirs. It's wavy and messy, like he's just begging for someone—*namely, me*—to run their fingers through it.

He wears a T-shirt so tight he might as well have painted it on, and his arms are covered in more tattoos than a rock star with a red-lipped, wannabe pinup girl on his arm. But they're nice arms, tanned and toned under the ink. The rest of him's not bad either.

"What's he play?" Lauren asks, bringing me back to the present. "You still on a soccer kick?"

"Oils? Acrylics? I'm not sure."

There's a long pause on the other side of the line. "Riley, those don't pertain to any sports."

From the shade of the gazebo, inconspicuous in

the crowd, I give him another once over. "I don't think he's a sports kind of guy."

"Well, look at you, branching out."

I smile, ready to branch out a little more. "I'm going to introduce myself."

"You haven't even met him yet?"

Even though she can't see me, I shrug. "I'm about to remedy that."

She laughs. "Call me later."

"Will do." I slide my phone into my back pocket, give my hair a toss, and stride forward, onto the grass where the vendors have set up their tents.

The Artisan Festival runs weekly in the summer months. Every Saturday, people come from all over Montana to hawk not only pieces of fine art but other crafts as well. There is a plethora of scrap metal sculptures, sliced sandstone plaques, hand-wrapped fine jewelry, and batik-died fabrics. There are even some cotton ball sheep and crocheted toilet paper cozies.

On the edges of the park, food vendors have set up their trailers, and families wander about, drinking lemonade, eating funnel cakes, and directing their small children away from the lady who sells hand-blown glass.

With the wildflowers, fresh cut grass, and the scent of sunscreen hanging in the air, it smells like summer.

I'm weaving through the crowd, halfway to the artsy Adonis's canopy, when a guy backs right into me. He stops and jumps forward, craning his head backward, apologetic. "Oh, sorry…"

He trails off as he likely realizes I'm not a thirty-something woman towing about a passel of children. The guy's good-looking enough but has small town written all over him. With floppy, sandy hair and nondescript eyes that might be blue or gray or even light brown, he could get lost in a crowd of five.

"Sorry," he says again, and this time his mouth stretches into a smile.

I stand on my tiptoes, looking over his shoulder, and try to step around him. "No worries."

"I'm Linus."

A girl with an enviable hourglass figure sidles up to my artist. She's pointing at his work, and he's lapping up her attention.

Oh, great. Now she's touching his arm.

Irritated, I glance back at the guy who's watching me. He's just waiting for me to do the polite thing and introduce myself. On any other day, I'd smile, maybe flirt a tiny bit just for the fun of it, but now my tall, dark, and handsome is reaching for the girl's phone.

"No!" I say under my breath, horrified.

The guy in front of me raises his eyebrows and

glances over his shoulder. When he turns back, a wry frown replaces his smile.

The artist calls for his neighbor to watch his stand, and he walks off with the girl.

With a huff of defeat, I cross my arms and finally turn my attention back to the-boy-who-doesn't-know-when-to-move-along. "Riley."

"You new here?" Apparently not the type to give up easily, he's like one of those scrappy dogs used to working for attention.

"My aunt lives here," I say. "I'm visiting for the summer."

He nods, and his smile slowly returns. "I grew up here."

"That's..." I have nothing. Lamely, I finish, "Awesome."

After a moment, he rolls his eyes, lets out a mirthless laugh under his breath, and jerks his chin toward the deserted art stand. "His name is Zeke."

"You know him?" The words come out way too excited, and I attempt to school my features so I don't look quite so interested.

"Sure." Linus clasps his hands behind his head. "Small town. We all pretty much grew up together."

"So he lives here?"

He shakes his head. "No, but he comes back during the summer for the festivals."

I process the information, and my eyes drift to Linus's T-shirt. It's gray, skims over his lean-muscled shoulders and chest, and a pixelated, blocky green character stretches across the front.

"?" I motion to the block print over the image. "What does that mean exactly?"

A quick smile flashes over his face. "I'm gonna take a guess and say you're not a video game kind of girl."

"*Ew, no*," I say before I can stop myself, and then I cringe.

He only laughs and waves to a shop across the road from the park. "I'm working at the video game store this summer."

I eye him. So he's a geek.

He doesn't exactly look geekish. He's not scrawny or awkward. But facts are facts.

"Sorry," I apologize, hoping I didn't offend him, though it comes out sounding more like I'm sorry he's such a loser.

Linus shrugs. "So I'll see you around?"

"Sure." I'm barely able to pay attention because Zeke has walked back—and he's alone. Just to be friendly, I flash Linus a quick smile as I hurry past him. "Nice to meet you."

"You too," he calls, but I've already moved on.

As I make my way toward the canopy, I straighten

my posture and put on a serious look. Without even glancing at the impossibly handsome, dark-haired artist, I browse his paintings.

They're bold, thoughtful...have a brooding vibe to them. Honestly, they look a lot like the finger paint masterpieces a preschooler I used to babysit would ask me to hang on her parents' fridge.

But that probably means something. Something deep—something I'm gonna have to figure out real quick because out of the corner of my eye, I see Zeke walking my way.

Once he reaches me, he crosses his arms and studies a painting right along with me. "What do you see?"

What I *see* is a glob of red plastered over a lake-like splodge of blue. There's some yellow in there that looks like it was splattered on with a toothbrush. What I *say* is, "It's raw, emotional. The primary colors make me think of the elementary basics of life."

Lies. All lies.

Zeke looks my way and studies me with an intent expression on his face. "That's amazing. I was in a vulnerable state while painting this, but I haven't been able to peg the emotion behind it—it was just this ache, you know? And you just..." He shakes his head, and an approving smile tilts his lips. "Awesome."

Vulnerable state.

Okay, I'm going to be honest. I don't know what to do with that statement. I shrug, trying to look modest when, really, I hope he doesn't see right through me.

Now would be a good time to explain something about myself. I'm not exactly an artsy kind of girl. In high school, I steered clear of the art room unless Lauren dragged me in there. The closest I've ever been to fine art is those reproduction prints they hang in hotels.

I'm art inept, and in the last eighteen years of my life, I've been happy to be that way.

That's why, when Zeke says, "So are you an artist yourself?" I freeze.

"No." My voice goes up an octave. But he looks so disappointed, I blurt out, "I'm more of a crafter."

No. No, I'm not. I can't even work a glue gun.

Zeke leans against his table and crosses his arms. His tattoo-covered muscles bulge—actually *bulge*. "Yeah? What do you craft?"

Subtly, my eyes dart around for inspiration. Quilts?

No way—I accidentally sewed over my finger when Grandma tried to teach me how to make a pot holder.

Doll clothes? Paper mache? Gum wrapper origami?

What am I going to say?

"Soap."

Soap?

It's the first thing that comes to mind. Lauren's made it a few times, but I've never actually watched the process.

He nods like it's a reasonable answer. "I've known a few people who make it. Do you process it? Or do you prefer the melt and pour?"

He says "melt and pour" with such disdain that I answer, "Um...process?"

"Do you do candles too?"

Sure, why not.

I give him an easy smile. "Of course."

After all, if you're going to dig the hole, you might as well make it a deep one.

"You should talk to Linda." He nods toward a woman at the booth toward the front of the event. "See about setting up a table."

Never going to happen.

"Yeah?"

He jerks his chin up in a nod, and there's a wolfish glint in his eyes. "Absolutely—though my motives are fairly selfish."

I cock my hip, pleased. "Why's that?"

Zeke gives me a slow-burning sort of smirk. "If you're working alongside me, I might look forward to getting up early on Saturdays."

And like an idiot, I lean forward, look up at him

from under my eyelashes, and say, "Well, then...I better go talk to Linda."

About the Author

Shari L. Tapscott writes young adult fantasy and humorous contemporary fiction. When she's not writing or reading, she enjoys gardening, making soap, and pretending she can sing. She loves white chocolate mochas, furry animals, spending time with her family, and characters who refuse to behave.

Tapscott lives in western Colorado with her husband, son, daughter, and two very spoiled Saint Bernards.

To learn more about Shari's books, please visit: **shariltapscott.com**

Made in the USA
Monee, IL
19 November 2019

17094559R00182